GARBAGE PAIL KIDS™

WELCOME TO SMELLVILLE

BY
R.L. STINE

COMING SOON

More Garbage Pail Kids Books
by R.L. Stine

Illustrated by **JEFF ZAPATA**

Art Assistance by **FRED WHEATON**

AMULET BOOKS • NEW YORK

R.L. STINE

GARBAGE PAIL KIDS™

WELCOME TO SMELLVILLE

Cataloging-in-Publication Data has been applied for and may be obtained from the Library of Congress.

ISBN 978-1-4197-4361-0

Copyright © 2020 The Topps Company, Inc.

™ & © The Topps Company, Inc. All Rights Reserved. Garbage Pail Kids and GPK are registered trademarks of The Topps Company, Inc. and is officially licensed by The Topps Company, Inc.

Background artwork credits: Dirty Surface: Shutterstock/garmoncheg; Notebook: Shutterstock/Pixfiction; Clipboard: Shutterstock/NWM

By R.L. Stine
Interior illustrations by Jeff Zapata
Art assistance by Fred Wheaton
Cover art by Joe Simko
Book design by Brenda E. Angelilli

Printed and bound in the United States
10 9 8 7 6 5 4 3 2

Amulet Books are available at special discounts when purchased in quantity for premiums and promotions as well as fundraising or educational use. Special editions can also be created to specification. For details, contact specialsales@abramsbooks.com or the address below.

Amulet Books® is a registered trademark of Harry N. Abrams, Inc.

ABRAMS The Art of Books
195 Broadway, New York, NY 10007
abramsbooks.com

"We're not bad kids. We just don't know any better."

This book would have been left in the garbage pile if it weren't for the dedication and enthusiasm of my friend from Topps, Ira Friedman. Ira's Garbage Pail Kids expertise is at the top of the heap, and I couldn't have done it without him.

I'd also like to thank my thoughtful and caring editor, Charlie Kochman. Charlie scrupulously worked on this book as if he were editing Shakespeare (which it isn't).

A tip of the Unknown Sanitation Worker's cap to you both.

Meet the

GARBAGE PAIL KIDS™

ADAM BOMB

BABBLING BROOKE

BRAINY JANEY

CRANKY FRANKIE

HANDY SANDY

JUNKFOOD JOHN

LUKE PUKE

NERVOUS REX

ROB SLOB

WACKY JACKIE

ONE

Welcome to Smellville Middle School, everyone. I'm Adam Bomb and I'm about to *e-x-p-l-o-d-e* with excitement!

I'm here at the science fair in the gym to cheer on my friend Rob Slob. I think Rob is about to win first prize with his "Strange Minerals" display.

I had high hopes for *my* science project. It was a Rube Goldberg conveyor-belt machine for washing your cat.

A few minutes ago, Mrs. Hooping-Koff, our teacher, walked up to my display. "Let's see how it works."

"It's simple," I told her as I pulled a cat from a carton on the floor. "I attach the cat to this conveyor belt. The belt moves forward. Then soap and water pours out from this hose."

"Hey, that looks just like *my* cat!" Mrs. Hooping-Koff exclaimed.

"It *is* your cat," I said. "I don't have a cat."

"You should have asked me if you wanted to borrow Fluffy," she said.

"I asked Fluffy," I replied. "Fluffy seemed okay with it."

Mrs. Hooping-Koff did not seem okay with it.

I tied the cat to the conveyor belt. "Now watch this!" I said and flipped the switch. The belt started to move. Fluffy slid forward. Soapy water squirted from the hose.

"YAAAAAAAOWWWWWW!"

I saw the problem: The spin cycle was stuck.

"YAAAAAAAOWWWWWW!"

I flipped the switch again—but nothing happened.

"YAAAAAAAOWWWWWW!"

Mrs. Hooping-Koff started screaming. "Somebody help! *Heelllp!*"

It took three people to pull Fluffy out of the machine. She was okay, though. She still had a little fur on her body. Mostly on her legs.

"At least she's really clean!" I said.

Mrs. Hooping-Koff grabbed the cat and scowled at me. "Adam, don't ever speak to me again."

I knew she was joking. But I didn't really get the joke.

TWO

Our friend Handy Sandy had a good project, too. Her science entry was called "The Effects of Dropping Water Balloons on Teachers' Heads."

Sandy climbed up to the gym balcony and dropped colorful water balloons on our teachers.

PLOP! PLOP! SPLASSSSH! PLOP!

Ha ha! I never knew Sandy had such good aim!

It was a fun science experiment. But the teachers weren't impressed. Mrs. Hooping-Koff made Sandy get a towel and dry everyone off. She then had to sit in Principal Grunt's office for the rest of the day.

So...goodbye, Handy Sandy. She was out of the running.

Now I'm waiting with Rob Slob. Mrs. Hooping-Koff will come to Rob soon. Right now she is across the aisle, judging the project by Peter and Patty Perfect.

I can tell Rob Slob is nervous. He normally smells like garbage. But when he gets tense, he smells like garbage and a lot of other things you don't want to think about.

The poor guy can't help it. He thinks he'll take a bath sometime and maybe that will help.

Of course, Peter and Patty, the Perfect twins, have a perfect project. Rob Slob and I listened in as they explained it to Mrs. Hooping-Koff.

"We started out with an awesome idea," Peter explained. "We wanted to do a life-size model of our solar system."

"But our living room isn't big enough for that," Patty said. "So we brought it down in size a bit."

I studied their project. It had eight different-colored objects dangling on strings.

"This is the solar system," Peter Perfect said, twirling one of the planets on their mobile. "It's made entirely from fruit."

"And we used only *organic* fruit," Patty Perfect added proudly.

"This plum is the Earth," Peter explained. "And that lemon is Venus."

Mrs. Hooping-Koff nodded and wrapped her hand around another piece of fruit. "And what is this grapefruit?" she asked, picking it up from the table. "Uranus?"

"That's not part of the display," Patty replied. "We were saving it for lunch."

Mrs. Hooping-Koff scribbled some notes on her pad. "A wonderful project," she told the twins.

"We're going to donate all of the fruit to poor people," Peter said, grinning so that his perfect teeth gleamed in the gym lights.

"Wonderful," Mrs. Hooping-Koff muttered, and she scribbled some more on her pad.

Then she turned to our table. "One more project to judge," she said. "And then it's time to award first place . . . to the Perfect twins."

THREE

Mrs. Hooping-Koff walked up to Rob Slob's display. She sniffed the air and made a disgusted face.

People do that a lot when they get close to Rob. They can't help it. He stinks.

Our teacher gazed down at Rob's glass display case. "Hmmm . . ." she murmured and read the description he had printed out. "Strange Minerals."

Rob burped. "I've been collecting them for a long time," he told her.

Mrs. Hooping-Koff ran her finger along the top of the case, studying the little mineral deposits. "Wow, I like the green ones," she said. "And that purple one is quite unusual, too."

Rob grinned. "Thanks."

Our teacher wrapped her fingers around one and picked it up. She brought it close to her face, then sniffed. "And where does this brown mineral come from?"

"From my nose," Rob said. "I pulled them all from my nose. They're boogers."

The brown glob dropped from her hand, bounced on the table, and landed on the floor. Mrs. Hooping-Koff opened her mouth wide and a sound came out, something like **"GAAAAAACK."**

Then she covered her mouth and had the dry heaves.

"Does this mean I win?" Rob asked.

FOUR

Well, the Perfect twins won first place for their organic-fruit solar system mobile.

They win first place in everything because they're perfect.

I feel bad for Rob Slob. He worked hard on his science project. I'd seen him up late at night with a red, sore nose putting the finishing touches on his collection.

The poor guy was so disappointed, he began to eat some of his minerals.

Sad. But I couldn't stick around to cheer him up.

I am in a mad rush because my friends and I are in deep doo-doo right now. I mean, trouble spelled with a capital Y-I-K-E-S. And I have to get home and warn them before I explode.

What's wrong with ten kids living in a house all by ourselves? And who needs parents, anyway? Parents are total pains.

Am I right? (Just nod your head.)

Sure, we're messy and loud and crazy and we scream a lot and laugh like baboons and fight and throw things and ride our scooters on the roof and make rude sounds and don't smell great and paint things on people's garages.

But we're not bad kids. We just don't know any better.

So today I heard a rumor in school that Mr. and Mrs. Perfect, Peter and Patty's parents, are going to come to our house and check us out.

And if they find out we don't have parents ... it could be a *disaster*. We could lose our *house*. We could lose our *freedom*. We could even lose our soft-serve swirl ice-cream dispenser!

And where would we all go?

BOOOOOOM!

I told you, my name is Adam Bomb. And when I get tense and worried and angry, I burst apart and explode in all directions.

And it gets a little messy.

I leaped over a row of garbage cans and dodged the swarms of flies in our backyard. One of these

months we'll have to take the garbage out front to be picked up.

A few hundred flies followed me into the house as I tossed my backpack to the floor and burst into the living room. I was out of breath and sweat poured down my face.

Pooper, our big brown mutt, came running to greet me. He leaped up, put his paws on my shoulders, and licked the sweat off my face. He has a rough sandpaper tongue, and his licks burn.

Why do dogs like to lick so much?

"Good boy, Pooper. Good boy. Now get lost!"

I wrestled Pooper away and gazed around the room. "Is everyone here?" I cried. "Listen up. We have to talk. This is an EMERGENCY!"

FIVE

My friends were scattered around the living room. No one looked up.

Wacky Jackie, Rob Slob, and Junkfood John were staring at the TV watching their favorite superhero show, *Jonny Pantsfalldown*.

It's a pretty good show. I've watched it a few times. Although it always ends the same way: Jonny's pants fall down.

Jackie, Rob, and John laugh like lunatics at every episode. And they never guess the ending!

Nervous Rex was sitting by himself in a corner reading a book called *How to Calm Down in 30 Seconds*. I don't think it was working. The book was shaking in Rex's hands.

Brainy Janey sat on the edge of the couch staring into space. She's such a serious brainiac. I knew she was

thinking hard about something. Or maybe she was just pretending. How can you tell, when someone is as smart as Janey?

Handy Sandy had a soccer ball in her lap. The ball had lost a lot of air. She was trying to repair it with a wrench. Sometimes Sandy isn't as handy as she thinks she is.

"Listen up!" I screamed. "Come on. Listen to me. We need to talk!"

Wacky Jackie and Junkfood John giggled at the TV screen. John had a big snack bowl on his lap. His favorite snack is pretzel-covered pretzels. But John will snack on just about anything. I once saw him gobble up mouse droppings off the carpet. It's really hard to unsee something like that.

"PLEASE! LISTEN TO ME!" I screamed.

A few heads turned toward me.

"Shut your yap!" Cranky Frankie shouted. He was just being Cranky Frankie. That's his favorite expression. He even says it when he wakes up in the morning.

I realized we weren't all here. "Where is Luke Puke?" I asked. "Anyone see Luke?"

"He had a hurling match after school," Handy Sandy said.

Luke is a star of the hurling team. The team is in the citywide Competitive Puking League.

Luke Puke has been puking since he was a little kid. Coach Swettypants says Luke could be an all-state champ in the 300-meter projectile event.

Most hurlers warm up by sticking their finger down their throat. But give Luke a good punch in the stomach and he's ready to compete. He's a great athlete. I've even seen him hurl on an empty stomach!

"Let me tell you what I heard," I started. But before I could go any further, Babbling Brooke came bursting into the room.

"I've got to get back to school," she said. "I have cheerleader tryouts for the hurling team."

"Shut your yap," Cranky Frankie muttered.

"How can you be a hurling team cheerleader?" Brainy Janey asked. "They don't allow anyone to watch the matches."

"Why?" Brooke demanded.

"Because as soon as the team starts to puke, the audience joins in. They can't help themselves."

"I don't care," Brooke said. "They need cheerleaders."

I took a deep breath. "Please, everyone—listen to me!" I repeated. "I have something important to tell you!"

"Let me show you my team cheers," Brooke said. "Everybody stand back. What do you think of this one? I wrote it myself."

She raised her hands above her head and began to jump and cheer:

"SMELLVILLE, SMELLVILLE, WE'RE SO HOT!
"GO AHEAD, HURLERS. GIVE 'EM ALL YOU GOT!"

That cheer ended in a split. Brooke quickly picked herself up. Breathing hard, she leaped into the air and began a second cheer:

"GO SMELLVILLE! GO SMELLVILLE!
"OUR HURLERS ARE THE TOP!
"WHEN WE LEAVE THE ROOM,
"YOU'LL NEED MORE THAN ONE MOP!"

Brooke wiped sweat off her forehead with the back of one hand. Then she grinned at me. "Adam, what do you think?"

"I think we're all in serious trouble," I said. "Let me tell you what I heard in school today. I heard that Mr. and Mrs. Perfect are coming to our house. I think—"

But that's as far as I got.

I stopped when I heard a loud, hard knock on the front door.

"It's the Perfects!" I cried. "We're dead meat!"

SIX

Hi, I'm Brainy Janey. I'm going to pick up the story from here and tell you what happened.

Earlier that day, Mrs. Hooping-Koff called on me in class to do my science demonstration. I was ready. I carried my brain to the front of the room and set it down on her desk.

I had practiced my talk at home to Wacky Jackie the day before. She didn't understand it at all. So I knew it was good.

I took a deep breath and turned to the class. "My science project is about the human brain," I said, and rubbed my hand over the top of the brain.

Nervous Rex raised his hand. I could see he was shaking. "Th-that's not a real brain—is it?" he stammered. He lowered his hand and chewed his fingernails.

I shook my head. "No, it's a life-size model I made."

"That's not life-size for Cranky Frankie," Luke Puke interrupted. "You need a magnifying glass to find his!"

"You're *sitting* on *your* brain!" Frankie shouted back.

"Hey, everyone, could you let Janey give her report? I'm really interested in it," Peter Perfect said.

As we all know, Peter and his sister Patty are perfect in every way.

That's why everyone hates them.

"Thank you, Peter," Mrs. Hooping-Koff said, flashing him a warm smile. "Janey, I know we're all looking forward to picking your brain on the subject."

"You don't pick your brain. You pick your nose!" Rob Slob said.

No one laughed.

Nervous Rex raised his hand again. I noticed he'd chewed all ten of his fingernails. "Are you sure that brain isn't r-real?"

"I made it out of Play-Doh," I said. "It's just a model, Rex."

"Rex, do you need a time out?" Mrs. Hooping-Koff asked. "You're shaking."

"N-n-n-no, I'm not," he insisted. "The ceiling fan is shaking. Not me!"

"Please continue, Janey," Mrs. Hooping-Koff said. "Tell us what you learned about the brain."

I turned the brain around so everyone could see the ridges and valleys I had carved into it. "Let's start here at the top," I said. I rubbed my hand over the largest section. "The brain is divided into different sections. This is called the *metamucil ablagabla.*"

"Those are interesting words," Mrs. Hooping-Koff said, gazing at my brain.

"I believe they are pig latin," I said. "All the early scientists used pig latin to name things in the old days."

"I'm not so sure about that, but go on," our teacher said. "I hope everyone is taking notes. There will be a quiz later."

I rubbed my finger down the jagged line I had carved into the side of my model. "This is where the *hippocrampulus* meets the *abadaba,*" I explained.

"And where is the human memory located?" Patty Perfect asked. She always asks the most perfect questions.

"Your memory cells are back here," I said, turning the brain around. "They're in the *lollapalooza* area. Your memories travel from all the way back here to your mouth."

"And where do headaches come from?" Patty Perfect asked.

"You give *me* a headache!" Cranky Frankie exclaimed. "Why don't you shut your yap?"

"Frankie, try not to be like yourself," Mrs. Hooping-Koff scolded.

"You get headaches when your *lollapalooza* is bumped or jolted in some way," I explained.

"You have to be careful with your brain," I continued. "It fits very snugly against your skull. And if your skull gets bumped really hard, the brain can come loose and drain down the back of your neck. That's called brain drain, and it's very dangerous."

SEVEN

Wacky Jackie reached out and tapped the top of Cranky Frankie's head three times with her fist. "Hear that? It's hollow! Brain drain! Definitely brain drain!"

Frankie slapped Jackie's hand away. "I'm smarter than you *without* a brain!" he exclaimed. "Your IQ is so low, it's a *minus zero*! You have to stay up and study all night to be able to find your socks in the morning!"

Jackie turned to Mrs. Hooping-Koff. "Did that make any sense?"

"No, not really," Mrs. Hooping-Koff replied. She turned to me. "Good work, Janey. You've done a lot of research . . . I think."

I nodded. "I didn't just read articles. I also read the captions that were with the photographs."

"Impressive," our teacher said. "Please go on. I understand you have a demonstration."

"Yes, I brought something for everyone to try," I said.

"Did you bring Wacky Jackie a new brain?" Luke Puke shouted.

Jackie swung around to face him. "I don't need a brain to punch your lights out!"

Luke laughed. "I'm not scared of you."

"You *should* be!" Jackie shot a fist to his forehead, and his head wobbled around like a bobblehead doll.

Mrs. Hooping-Koff moved quickly down the row of desks—and gave Jackie a hard pinch on the cheek.

PINNNNNCH.

"No violence!" she cried. "No violence in my class! No violence or I'll pinch you till you faint!"

She's a big believer in nonviolence.

"I gave him a love tap," Jackie said softly. "I was just messing with him."

Luke had a hand over his mouth. "May I be excused? I think I'm going to—" And he ran out of the room.

"Janey, please continue," Mrs. Hooping-Koff said.

"I brought everyone a brain today," I said. "Actually, a small piece of a brain. You know, some people *eat* brains."

There were a lot of groans and laughs.

"No, really," I said. "Once, in a fancy restaurant, I ate a big plate of brains."

Nervous Rex made a gasping sound. "Did it make you sick?"

"Of course not," I said.

"I'll bet it tasted just like chicken," Babbling Brooke said.

"No," I explained. "It tasted just like brains."

That got a lot of **EEEW**s and **YUCK**s.

I walked to the back of the room and picked up the platter I had brought. "Here you go," I said. "I have a little piece of brain for everyone. Taste it and see what you think."

EIGHT

I had already cut the sections of brain into little squares, and I placed a piece on every desk as I made my way down the aisle.

Patty Perfect raised her hand and waved to the teacher. "Mrs. Hooping-Koff, if we eat the brain, do we get extra credit?"

The Perfect twins want extra credit for everything they do. Peter Perfect once asked if he could have extra credit for going to the bathroom.

"I think Janey should get extra credit for bringing in treats for us to snack on," Mrs. Hooping-Koff said, flashing me another smile. "Let's all sample ours at the count of three, class. One . . . two . . . three."

I watched as everyone popped the little squares into their mouths and started to chew.

Mrs. Hooping-Koff swallowed hers with a loud **GULP.** Then she turned to me. "What kind of brains was that, dear?"

"From my Uncle Henry. He died last week."

Mrs. Hooping-Koff's mouth dropped open in a groan of horror. "Ohhh noooo!"

The class erupted in wails and moans. Kids pressed their hands over their mouths and gagged. A few kids ran out of the room, choking.

I laughed. "Kidding! Just kidding!" I shouted over the uproar. "I was just messing with you!"

I may be a brainiac, but I like to have fun, too.

"They are actually potatoes!" I confessed.

Everyone was gagging and screaming and carrying on so loudly, I wasn't sure they heard me.

"Potatoes!" I shouted. "Potatoes!"

I grabbed a square off the tray and popped it into my mouth to show them. They finally started to settle down, but they weren't laughing.

After school, I walked home with Babbling Brooke. Brooke wants to be a cheerleader and was practicing cheers in her head.

Pooper greeted us at the front door, wagging his big tail and jumping up, trying to knock us over. Wacky Jackie and Junkfood John were already sprawled on the

couch watching an episode of that superhero show they like, *Jonny Pantsfalldown*.

We were all just hanging out when Adam Bomb came bursting into the house. He looked about ready to explode.

"I think we're all in serious trouble!" Adam shouted. "Let me tell you what I heard in school today." He was red-faced and balloon-eyed and frantic.

"I heard that Mr. and Mrs. Perfect are coming to our house," he cried. "I think—"

Then there was a loud knock on the front door.

Adam's face went from tomato red to milk white. "It's the Perfects!" he cried. "We're dead meat!"

NINE

I'm Cranky Frankie. Let me tell you what *really* happened...

I knocked on the door three times and no one came to open it.

I muttered some nasty words under my breath.

What were they trying to do, keep me out? Just because once in a while I lose my temper and use a few bad words?

Those bird-brained, pig-headed, jerk-faced sloth buckets know how much I like them. The dunder-faced idiots are my buddies—my best friends in the whole world. I wouldn't hurt their feelings for anything...if I could help it.

I knocked again.

I could hear Adam Bomb's voice shouting something about the neighbors. And I could hear *Jonny Pantsfalldown* on the TV.

Yeah, I had been there in the living room with them before. But I had to get out when Babbling Brooke started doing her cheers. I've been asked not to say anything bad about her cheerleading ability. So I don't say anything.

I took a walk around the block, and when I came back, they wouldn't let me in.

I knocked a fourth time, and finally Adam opened the front door.

He gawked at me like he'd never seen me before. "Oh, it's you!" he cried.

"No, it's Bazooka Joe," I said, and pushed past him and into the house. Everyone was in the living room. They all looked shocked.

"Don't stare at me like bug-eyed toads," I said. "I live here, too, you know."

"Wh-why did you knock?" Adam stammered. He still looked pale and shaky.

"I forgot my key," I said.

"We don't use keys," Adam replied. "The door is always open."

"Oh, I forgot," I said.

I turned around and Luke Puke followed me into the house.

"Why are you back so soon?" I demanded. "I thought you had a hurling match at school."

Luke frowned at me. "Coach Swettypants sent me home. He said I couldn't puke with the team today."

Adam blinked. "Why?"

"Because I have an upset stomach."

Adam nodded. "That makes sense."

"Do you know the cure for an upset stomach?" Handy Sandy asked.

Luke turned to her. "No, what?"

She shrugged. "I don't know. I was asking you."

I wrestled Junkfood John to the floor and took

his place on the couch. Then I grabbed his bowl of pretzel-covered pretzels and finished them off for him. I even chewed the last one right in his face so he could see how much I was enjoying it.

"Help yourself to my pretzels, Frankie," he said. I think he was being sarcastic, but I didn't pay any attention.

Babbling Brooke came striding to the center of the room. She smiled at Luke and said, "I've been practicing some new cheers. I'm going to be a cheerleader for your hurling team."

"Brooke, we don't have time—" Adam said.

But she leaped into the air, swung her hands high, and began the cheer anyway.

"HURL IT UP! HURL IT UP! WAAAAY UP!

"SMELLVILLE IS GONNA ROCK YOU.

"SMELLVILLE IS GONNA SHOCK YOU.

"DA DA DA DADADA DA DA! DA DA DA DA.

"YAAAAAY!"

She clapped her hands and finished with a split. Then she grinned. "What do you think, Luke?"

"Brooke," Luke said, "what are all the 'da da da's at the end?"

"I haven't finished it," she replied. "But do you like it?"

I spoke up before Luke could answer. "I like it as much as pounding a six-inch nail into my forehead."

"Oh, thank you!" she cried happily, clapping her hands.

TEN

I'm Luke Puke. My turn now ...

Pooper, stretched out on his stomach against the wall, raised his head and groaned. I don't think he liked Brooke's cheer, either.

"Ptooey!" called a shrill voice. **"Ptooey!"**

That's our other pet, a fat smelly parrot named Ptooey. He loves saying his name over and over.

That's not all he says. He thinks he's some kind of insult comedian. Actually, he's just nasty. I don't like to go near his cage because he bites.

"Ptooey, why don't you shut your yap?" Cranky Frankie shouted.

"Why don't you swallow your head?" the parrot squawked back. **"Swallow your head! Swallow your head!"**

"Somebody pull the cover over his cage," Adam Bomb said.

"Not me," Nervous Rex said. "The last time I went up to his cage, he bit my middle finger off."

I squinted at him. "Let me see your hand."

Rex held it up.

"How'd you get the finger back on?" I asked.

"Kwazy Glue."

"Ptooey! Ptooey!" the parrot squawked. **"Come near me again, I'll peck your face off. Try me!"**

"How did we get that featherbrain, anyway?" I asked.

Silence.

"No one knows," Rob Slob said.

We all turned to Brainy Janey. She's the brainiest brainiac in the house. She knows everything.

"Do you know how we got the parrot?" I asked.

She shook her head. "No, I don't."

"Do you know how we got our dog, Pooper?" Adam asked.

Janey shook her head. "No, I don't."

"We don't know anything about ourselves," Handy Sandy said. "Janey, do you know how we all got here in this house?"

Janey shook her head. "No, I don't."

"Well then, how did we all get to Smellville?" Sandy asked. "Do you know?"

Janey shook her head. "No, I don't."

"Why don't we have parents?" Brooke chimed in. "And why do we live here all by ourselves?"

"I don't know," Janey said.

"Why are we all sort of . . . different?" Wacky Jackie asked. "How come we're not like the other kids? Do you know?"

Janey shook her head. "No, I don't."

"We're not getting anywhere," I said. "Enough with the questions."

Brainy Janey turned to me. "If we don't ask questions, how are we going to learn anything?"

JONNY PANTSFALLDOWN

Favorite TV superhero of Wacky Jackie and Junkfood John
Episode 233

Keep the faith, everyone! And keep your belt buckled tight for ADVENTURE! It's time for another thrilling episode of JONNY PANTSFALL-DOWN, told by me, the world's greatest sidekick—THE MIGHTY HAIRBALL!

"I will never let you down!"

That's what Johnny Pantsfalldown promised the good people of Pupick Falls.

And he always keeps his word.

Every night, after a healthy dinner of fish parts and lo mein, Jonny puts on his cape, his mask, and his Pants of Steel. Then, side by side with me—the Mighty

Hairball—he fights crime and terrifies criminals with his famous battle cry:

"YODEL-AY-EEE-OOOO!"

Tonight, I found Jonny pulling on his costume in his secret dressing room high above the cliffs of Pupick Falls. He struggled with the mask. I saw that he had the eyeholes in the back, and I helped him turn his mask around.

"How strange. I can see much better with the eyeholes in the front," he said in the deep booming voice that makes evildoers' ears bleed. Jonny's eyes burned into mine. "Hairball, did you bring the suspenders I asked for?"

"GULP."

I made a loud gulping sound. I like to brag that I gulp better than any other sidekick in the superhero universe. My secret: I practice gulping in my room.

"Sorry, Jonny," I said. "I forgot your suspenders."

"No worries," he boomed, pulling his Pants of Steel higher on his impressive hips. "Tonight, nothing can hold up my path to victory."

"What criminal are we chasing tonight?" I asked, adjusting the spandex underpants I wear on the outside of my costume.

"Tonight, we will bring down Big Bootus," Jonny announced. "Big Bootus will attempt to rob twelve-year-old Shirley Ba-Birley's piggy bank right off her bedroom dresser."

I blinked. "Big Bootus plans to rob a piggy bank?"

Jonny nodded. "Shirley Ba-Birley is an amazing finder of quarters and nickels on the sidewalk. So far, she has tucked away two million dollars in her piggy bank—and Big Bootus knows it."

"Wowser." I shook my head in awe. "Jonny, how do you always know how to find Big Bootus?"

"It's easy," Jonny said. "He has the biggest bootus in town."

JONNY PANTSFALLDOWN CONTINUED...

We took off into the night. Jonny's pants fluttered in the wind as he soared higher into the purple sky. When the wings of my battle helmet started to flap in the breeze, I sailed up after him.

The moon rose to meet us and cast its white light on the houses down below. I had to remind myself not to look down. I'm afraid of heights.

Jonny pointed to a long ranch house down below. "That's Shirley Ba-Birley's house," he boomed. His voice is so deep it knocked over a few trees.

Jonny swooped down and landed on the grass of the backyard.

"YOWCCH." I dropped down hard into a metal wheel-barrow. I felt several bones in my legs crack.

A good reminder to practice my landings.

Both legs were broken. A minor injury for the Mighty Hairball. I couldn't let Jonny know I was hurt. He depends on me.

I scrambled out of the wheelbarrow and crawled across the grass toward Shirley's house.

It was completely dark. The windows were black and appeared to gaze out at us . . . like black windows gazing out.

"Big Bootus is already inside," Jonny whispered. "Shirley's room is at the top of the stairs. We'll creep up and catch him in the act."

"Sounds like a plan," I said.

"Trust me, he won't get his hands on the two million dollars in that piggy bank," Jonny whispered.

I followed him onto the back stoop.

He tried the door.

"Locked."

He shook his head sadly.

"Now what do we do? I'm stumped."

"Try the front door?" I suggested.

Jonny sighed. "It's probably locked, too."

He shook his head again. "Defeated. We're defeated, Hairball."

We both stared at the locked door.

"Did you happen to bring any door keys with you?" Jonny asked.

I shook my head. "No . . . sorry."

That's when I spotted an open window a few inches in front of Jonny's face and pointed. "Jonny, look. A window."

"Brilliant!" he cried. "An open window. It just goes to show, Hairball, that you should never give up hope."

A few seconds later, we were in the kitchen. Slowly we peered around in the darkness.

My X-ray nose went into action. I gave several long, hard sniffs. "My X-ray nose tells me they had roast beef for dinner," I whispered.

"Good work, Hairball." Jonny tried to pat me on the back, but he missed. It was crazy dark in there.

"Let's move," he whispered. "Let's get upstairs to Shirley's room before Big Bootus can get his hands on that piggy bank."

JONNY PANTSFALLDOWN CONTINUED...

We started to race through the darkness.
CLANNNNNG!

I ran headfirst into the refrigerator.

The pain paralyzed me for a few seconds, then I pulled out a pad and pencil. "I'm making a note to bring a flashlight next time," I said.

"I like the way you think," Jonny whispered.

I followed him into the next room. My X-ray nose told me that someone had gone to the bathroom recently.

"We've got to find the stairs, pronto," Jonny whispered. "Big Bootus has a head start on us. We can't let him leave."

Stumbling in the dark, we circled the room. There was no stairway.

"Follow me," Jonny whispered, and we found ourselves in a long hallway. Silently, we crept on tiptoes so we wouldn't wake anyone up. "I don't see a stairway in this hall," Jonny said.

We doubled back and started in the kitchen again. Then we tried the dining room and the living room.

"How strange," Jonny said. He stopped short and I walked right into him. "No stairway anywhere. How does Shirley Ba-Birley get to her room?"

My brain was spinning. "I think I know what the problem is," I said. "We're in the wrong house."

"Brilliant!" Jonny cried. "I love how your mind works!"

I could feel myself blushing.

"Hurry," Jonny urged. He darted to the kitchen door and tried the knob. "Locked," he said. "We're locked in."

"Try the window," I said.

A few seconds later, we were standing in the backyard.

We heard the thudding footsteps coming from next door. And when we turned, we saw Big Bootus come bouncing around the side of the house.

The piggy bank, tightly gripped in his hands, gleamed in the moonlight.

"Stop right there!" Jonny boomed. "You'll never get away with that piggy bank!"

Big Bootus tossed his head back and laughed. "Jonny, your deep voice may have just given me a chill. But I'll bet my big bootus you can't catch me!"

The race was on.

"**YODEL-AY-eee-oooo!**" Jonny shouted his famous battle cry. Then he lowered his shoulder like a football running back and took off after the criminal.

Big Bootus's boots thudded the grass as he rocketed across the yard.

"You're catching up, Jonny!" I shouted. "You're gonna get him!" But then I saw Jonny's pants start to slip.

Jonny made a grab for them. Too late.

His Pants of Steel dropped down around his knees. He tripped over them, staggered, and fell face down on the driveway.

When Jonny sat up, he had gravel in his teeth. "If I only had those suspenders," he said sadly.

We watched Big Bootus disappear down the street with the two-million-dollar piggy bank.

"I'll get you next time!" Jonny yelled. "Or my name isn't Jonny Pantsfalldown!"

That's our exciting adventure for today, boys and girls. Until next time, this is the Mighty Hairball saying: "Keep your pants up—and reach for the stars!"

ELEVEN

It's me again, Brainy Janey. I'll take it from here . . .

Adam Bomb grabbed the TV remote from Wacky Jackie's hand and clicked off the TV.

Jackie tried to grab it back. "Why'd you turn it off?" she demanded. "There's another *Jonny Pantsfalldown* coming on after the commercial."

"This is the episode where his pants fall *up!*" Junkfood John said. "It's a riot."

Adam was red in the face. "I'm trying to explain to you we have a real emergency on our hands. If Mr. and Mrs. Perfect find out we have no parents here, we'll all be sent away. We'll lose everything."

Babbling Brooke chimed in. "Do you think they'll send us someplace nice? Like Pupick Falls?"

"No," I said. "They'll split us up, Brooke. The city of

Smellville will find homes for us. We'll never see each other again."

"Do you promise?" Cranky Frankie said. Then he added, "Joking. Just joking. Man, everyone's a critic."

We're all used to Cranky Frankie's jokes. They're not funny at all.

Junkfood John jumped up from the couch. "I'm going to the kitchen for some snacks," he said.

"Could you bring me the bag of Fruit Smash-Ups?" Handy Sandy asked.

"I already smashed them and ate them," Junkfood John replied. He then burped the alphabet.

Adam Bomb grabbed John and pulled him back to the couch. "We don't have time for snacks," he said. "The Perfects will be here any minute."

We all turned to the door. Silence. No one was knocking.

"Adam is right," I said. "We need to have a meeting right now. I'm sure we can put our heads together and think of a way to stop the Perfects."

It got quiet, and everyone was staring at me. "Not literally," I explained. "We need to *brainstorm* and come up with a plan."

"All this talk is making me nervous," said Nervous Rex. He sat on the floor clinging to Pooper as if he was drowning and the dog was a life preserver.

"You've got to calm down, Rex," I said. "You even tremble and shake when you're asleep."

"My dreams make me nervous," he said.

"What do you dream?" I asked.

"I always dream that I'm nervous."

"Well, this isn't a dream," Adam interrupted. "The Perfects are real."

"I heard their dog barking this afternoon," Babbling Brooke said.

"No you didn't," Adam said. "Why do you think they named their dog Good Boy? He's so good, he only barks if they ask him to."

"Adam is right," I said. "The dog really is perfect. When they give him a dog biscuit, he says grace before he eats it."

The Perfects have two pets: Good Boy, the dog. And their cat, Mister Purrfect.

I know, yucky name, right?

"So let's all think," I said. "How can we keep the Perfects from finding out we don't have any parents?"

TWELVE

The room grew quiet as everyone tried to think.

"We could blindfold the Perfects when they come over?" Wacky Jackie suggested.

"That would work!" Babbling Brooke babbled.

"Please don't make me say that's the stupidest thing I ever heard," Cranky Frankie said.

"Go ahead ... say it," I replied.

Frankie took a breath. "That's the stupidest thing I ever heard."

"If we all stood on our heads," Wacky Jackie said, "they'd be so confused, they wouldn't know if we had parents or not."

"Please don't make me say *that's* the stupidest thing I ever heard," Cranky Frankie repeated.

"It's easy to criticize," Jackie sneered.

"Let me put my brainiac brain to work," I said. "I know I can come up with a good plan."

I shut my eyes. I gritted my teeth. I held my breath. And I let my brain go to work.

A few minutes later, I opened my eyes. "I've got it," I said.

Adam Bomb settled down on the couch next to Wacky Jackie and Junkfood John. "I knew brainiac here would save us," he said. "What's your plan?"

"Easy," I said. "We go to the costume store. And two of us will dress as grown-ups."

A hush fell over the room. Everyone was squinting at me.

"There is no costume store in Smellville," Adam said finally.

"And we're all too short," Brooke added. "We're kid-size."

"A grown-up costume wouldn't fit any of us. It would just fall off,'" Jackie said.

I shrugged. "Okay, okay. I admit it. There are a few flaws to my plan."

"We have to surrender," Nervous Rex said, biting his fingernails. "We have to give up. We don't stand a chance."

"Take a breath, Rex," Adam said.

"We're doomed!" Rex cried. "We're *doomed!*"

"Ptooey! Ptooey!" The parrot suddenly woke up on his perch against the window. **"I'll peck your guts out! Come over here! I'll peck your guts!"**

"Why do we keep that parrot?" Cranky Frankie moaned.

"Because he's so cute," Babbling Brooke gushed. "So cute and lovable. Look how he tilts his head from side to side. So adorable!"

"Come over here!" the parrot squawked. **"I'll give you a new nostril!"**

Suddenly, Junkfood John jumped to his feet. "I have it!" he shouted. "I have it!"

"What do you have?" I asked.

"I have a major stomachache!" he cried. **"ULLLLLP.** I shouldn't have eaten that whole bag of Fruit Smash-Ups!" Holding his belly, John went running to the bathroom.

"I think I have an idea." We all turned to Handy Sandy, who sat at the table, twirling a screwdriver between her hands.

"You know how to keep the Perfects away?" I asked.

Sandy nodded. "I've been experimenting with electricity," she said. "Trying a few things out. See this?" She held up a device with tangled wires and several large batteries.

"What's that for?" I asked.

"For shocking people," Sandy said. "See this electrode? I was going to attach it to Wacky Jackie. She's my lab partner in science class."

Jackie leaned forward on the couch. "You were going to attach that to *me*?"

Sandy nodded. "I wanted to do a test. You know. See how much electricity I could shoot into Jackie before she screamed and fell unconscious."

"Cool! That experiment would probably get us extra credit!" Jackie exclaimed.

"But, wait!" Handy Sandy exclaimed. She sucked on the screwdriver blade for a few moments. She's always putting tools in her mouth. It's pretty gross.

"What if . . ." Sandy started. "We used this little gadget to electrify the front doorknob?"

We all stared at her. We weren't sure what she meant to do.

"Anyone who touches the door knob gets zapped," Sandy said, a grin spreading over her face. "And I mean zapped. I'll fix it so a powerful *jolt* of electricity shocks whoever touches the knob. One shock and the Perfects will go running off—and they'll vibrate for a week."

"Brilliant!" I said. "That's the perfect way to treat our perfectly nosy neighbors, the Perfects."

Everyone agreed. So Handy Sandy went to work.

She spent hours wiring the doorknob. Attaching electrodes. Getting the power just right. Hiding the wires so no one could see them.

And wouldn't you know it? A few hours after Sandy finished, Mr. and Mrs. Perfect showed up.

We watched from the window as they approached our house.

We hid where they couldn't see us.

And we held our breath and waited for one of them to touch ... THE DOORKNOB OF DOOM.

THIRTEEN

Adam Bomb again. Allow me to continue the story from here ...

I felt so tense, I nearly exploded.

The Perfect twins, Peter and Patty, are bad news. But their parents, Parker and Penny Perfect, are a lot worse. They demand that Peter and Patty be perfect in every way.

Their pets have to be perfect, too. They even trained Mister Purrfect to stand up, salute, and purr "The Star-Spangled Banner."

We knew the Perfects didn't like being our neighbors. I'll be the first to admit it. We aren't exactly *perfect*.

We are noisy sometimes. We laugh a lot. We scream just for the fun of it.

Sometimes Wacky Jackie plays the bagpipes late at night when she can't sleep. Our house band, the Bleeding Scabs, often practices in the backyard at night.

For some reason, Pooper, our big lovable mutt, thinks the Perfects' front yard is a bathroom.

But that doesn't make us bad neighbors—*does it?*

And now here they were, snooping on us. Eager to see if we had any parents. Ready to have us thrown out of our own home just because we are on our own.

It wasn't fair.

And so, here I was, holding my breath along with everyone else. Waiting to hear the delightful **BUZZZZZZZZZ** that meant one of them had grabbed the doorknob and was receiving the shock of their life.

"Is anyone home?" I heard Parker Perfect shout from the front stoop.

"The door is open. Come on in!" I shouted back.

Here it comes . . . ! Here it comes . . . !

The front door swung open. And Penny Perfect stepped into the house, followed by her husband.

They had smiles on their tanned faces. But we knew the smiles were pasted on. And as they sniffed the air, their smiles faded quickly.

"Hello, everyone," Parker Perfect said.

We were all too stunned to answer.

The doorknob . . . I stared hard at it. The doorknob . . . It was a major fail.

Handy Sandy's face was bright red. She started to sputter and choke, then ran to the kitchen for a glass of water.

"How is everyone today?" Penny Perfect asked cheerily.

No one answered. We were all thinking the same thing. *Why weren't they running for their lives, shrieking in pain?*

"We came to speak to your parents," Parker Perfect said. "Are they home?"

"Ptooey! Come over here. I'll peck your eyes! I'll eat your eyeballs like olives!"

Both Perfects gasped and turned toward Ptooey.

Mr. Perfect pointed at the bird. "Is that your parrot? Did you teach him to say that?"

"We didn't teach him," I said. "He kinda learned it on his own."

"**Ptooey!**" The fat parrot lifted one scrawny bird leg and—**PLOP**—he pooped on the floor. We keep forgetting to put newspaper down.

"Could we speak to your mother or father?" Penny Perfect asked. I could see she was tense and didn't know what to do with her hands. She tried to shove them into her pockets, but she didn't have pockets.

"Would you like a snack?" Junkfood John asked. "I have a bag of oat balls I could bring out."

Mr. Perfect squinted up his face. "Oat balls?"

John nodded. "Yeah. They're awesome if you dip them in pork and beans."

"No, thank you," Parker Perfect said.

"I have clam bellies, too," Junkfood John said. "They're cold and a little slimy, but they still slide down your throat real good."

Mrs. Perfect covered her mouth with one hand. She had gone pale. Well, actually, her skin had become pale *green*.

"Your mother or father?" she asked, her voice suddenly weak.

"They're not home," Brainy Janey said. I could see Janey's brain had gone into high gear.

"Where are they?" Penny Perfect asked.

"They . . . had to go to the dentist," Janey said.

"The dentist? Both of them?" Mr. Perfect asked.

"Yes," Janey replied. "They had to have all their teeth pulled."

"Oh my goodness!" Mrs. Perfect cried. "That's horrible. Parker and I have perfect teeth. We go to the dentist once a week to have them checked. And they're always perfect."

"Why did they have *all* their teeth pulled?" Mr. Perfect asked.

Janey shrugged. "They just wanted to. For looks, I guess. They were having their piercings removed from their tongues, too."

Both Perfects looked sick now. Penny's chin was trembling. Parker kept swallowing hard.

"Well . . . we'll come back," Penny said, turning away. "We'll come visit them when they're over their . . . dental problems."

"Yes. Tell them we came by to say hi," Parker added.

The Perfects stumbled to the front of the house and quickly disappeared outside. The door closed hard behind them.

"Whew! That was close!" I cried.

"Way to go!" Babbling Brooke cried, and slapped Janey on the back. Janey and Junkfood John did a fist bump. "Go, Janey! Go, Janey!"

"I'm still shaking," Nervous Rex stammered. "Look at me. I can't stop sh-shaking." He shook so hard, he rolled out of his chair and lay trembling on the floor.

"They're gone. They couldn't wait to get out of here," I said. "Did you see the looks on their faces? Sick. They were sick!"

"Don't get too excited," Cranky Frankie said. "They'll be back."

Then we all turned to Handy Sandy.

"What happened?" I asked. "The doorknob? The great electrical shock that was supposed to send them away screaming?"

Sandy scratched her head. "Let me check."

She reached under the table and pulled up the control box. "Hmmmm hmmmm." Sandy hummed as she lowered her face close and examined it.

Finally, she looked up. "Wouldn't you know it?" she muttered. "I forgot to turn it on."

"You *what*?" I cried.

"I forgot to turn it on." She threw the switch and it made a loud click. "Now it's on. Watch," Sandy said.

She walked to the front door. Then wrapped her hand around the doorknob.

ZZZZZZZZZZZZZZZAAAAAAAAAAAAPP!
"YEEOWWWWWWWWWWWWWW!"

FOURTEEN

Nervous Rex here. I guess it's my turn to take over the story.

A week later, we were in school getting ready for art class.

Art class makes me nervous because I never know what to draw or paint or what to make. And I always think everyone else is better than me.

One day after class, I went up to Mrs. Hooping-Koff and told her how I felt. "I always think everyone is better than me," I said.

"Yes, everyone *is* better than you," she said. "But that doesn't mean you shouldn't do your best."

Those encouraging words meant a lot to me.

We were all sitting on wooden stools around a long table, waiting for Mrs. Hooping-Koff to hand out art supplies. Wacky Jackie stuck two paintbrushes in her nose. "Check it out. I'm a walrus," she said.

Cranky Frankie frowned at her. "Jackie, did anyone ever tell you you're a riot?" he asked.

Jackie shook her head. "No."

"Well, there's a reason," Frankie said. "Why don't you shut your yap?

Rob Slob had a runny nose. He *always* has a runny nose. "Does anyone have a tissue?" he asked. He had already dripped a big puddle of snot on the table in front of him.

"Just use the back of your hand," Wacky Jackie said. "That's what *I* do." She held up her hand, and it had a huge glob of green drippy stuff hanging from it.

"No one has a tissue? No problem," Rob Slob said, and wiped a glob of snot onto the front of Luke Puke's T-shirt.

Wacky Jackie turned to Babbling Brooke, who was sitting across the table from her. "Brooke, do you eat spaghetti with your right hand or your left hand?" she asked.

"My right hand," Brooke said. "Why?"

Jackie giggled. "That's funny. I use a *fork!*"

Everyone laughed. That was a pretty good joke.

Jokes make me nervous. I never know if they are funny or not. And then I don't know how long I should laugh.

I tried to tell a joke once. But I got too nervous to finish it and I had to run away.

Rob Slob made a disgusted face. "Where is that horrible smell coming from?"

"Can you spell Y-O-U?" Cranky Frankie said.

Rob sniffed both armpits. "No . . . it's not me."

He's so lucky. He can't smell his own odor.

"Get real! You stink!" Luke Puke cried.

Just then Mrs. Hooping-Koff came into the room. "You need to broaden your vocabulary, Luke," she said. "Rob doesn't stink. He has a *putrid aroma*."

"He has a putrid aroma that *stinks*!" Luke replied.

"That's much better," our teacher said.

FIFTEEN

Mrs. Hooping-Koff was carrying red and green square blocks, and she dropped one off in front of every student. "This is modeling clay," she said. "I thought we would work in clay today."

I picked up my clay and sniffed it. I liked the smell, but my hand started to shake.

"Do I have to?" I asked the teacher. "I don't think I'll be any good at it."

"I'm sure you won't be, Rex," Mrs. Hooping-Koff replied. "But you have to overcome your fear."

She frowned at me. "Look at you. Your hands are shaking."

"My hands are shaking, too!" Luke Puke cried and held up his hands. "Look. I have chills. I have to see the nurse."

"The nurse quit," Mrs. Hooping-Koff told him. "She said you made her sick."

"But I have the *chills*!" Luke insisted.

"Work with the clay," our teacher said. "It will warm you up."

"But clay gives me a rash," Luke said.

Mrs. Hooping-Koff ignored him. "Listen up, class," she said. "Soften the clay with your hands. Then form it into anything you want. Anything at all. I can't *wait* to see what you come up with."

Junkfood John raised his hand. "Mrs. Hooping-Koff, can I have another piece of clay?"

"Why do you need another piece of clay, John?"

"I ate mine," he said.

Junkfood John had green stuff on his lips and a chunk of clay stuck to his chin.

"Try not to eat this one, too," Mrs. Hooping-Koff said, giving him some more clay.

"Oh no. My nose dripped again," Rob Slob said. "My clay is all wet and sticky. Can I have another piece?"

Mrs. Hooping-Koff dropped another chunk of clay on the table in front of him. "Use a handkerchief, Slob," she said.

"I don't have one," Rob said. "But it's no problem." Then he pulled the front of Wacky Jackie's shirt to him and blew his nose into it.

We all worked with the clay for a while. My hands were shaking. I always get nervous when I can't decide what to make.

My clay slipped off the table and landed on top of my shoe. I tried to pull it off, but it stuck to the laces.

What if I can't get it off? What if everyone sees it and laughs at me? What if I can't walk?

I have a lot of nervous thoughts.

"Hey, check it out!" Wacky Jackie called, and held up her clay creation.

"What *is* that?" Mrs. Hooping-Koff asked.

Jackie grinned. "It's a body part! Guess what it is?"

"Put that away!" our teacher screamed. She grabbed it from Jackie's hands and frantically smushed it back into a ball.

Cranky Frankie chuckled. "Good one, Jackie."

The teacher stood behind Brainy Janey. "What are you making, Janey?"

Janey held up her clay. It was a perfect square cube.

"It's a pyramid," Janey said. "The ancient Egyptonians used modeling clay to build their pyramids."

"I'm not so sure about that," Mrs. Hooping-Koff said.

"I looked it up once," Janey replied. "I believe they kept their chariots inside the pyramids. You know. Like a garage. So the chariots wouldn't be out in the rain."

"Rain in the desert. Very interesting," our teacher said. "But, Janey, you're holding a cube. It isn't shaped like a pyramid."

"It's a *hidden* pyramid," Janey replied. "The Egyptonians hid their pyramids inside giant cubes so the pyramids wouldn't get wet."

She's such a brainiac.

It's no wonder she gets straight C-minuses on her report cards. Janey is tops in our class.

SIXTEEN

I know I'd do a lot better in school if I didn't get so nervous. Sometimes I'm so tense when I take a test, I chew *both* ends off my pencil. Then I have nothing to write with, and I just have to sit there while everyone else finishes.

Mrs. Hooping-Koff turned to me. "What did *you* make, Rex? Let me see it."

I held up my clay. It looked like a thin cigar.

"It's my favorite toy," I said. "A thermometer."

"Interesting," our teacher said.

Luke Puke grabbed the clay thermometer and jammed it into his mouth. He pulled it out quickly and read it. "I think I have a high fever," he said. "Can I see the nurse?"

"No. I told you, she quit," Mrs. Hooping-Koff repeated. "She said she was going home to stick pins into a voodoo doll she made of you."

Luke nodded. "That's sweet."

Across the table from me, Peter and Patty Perfect had been working silently on their projects. They both had their faces lowered to the art table. Their eyes narrowed, and their hands worked quickly, pushing and pulling at their clay.

Our teacher walked up behind them. "Let's see what you two have been working on so intently," she said.

Peter worked his clay a moment longer. Then he raised it off the table. "It's a stallion," he said. "You can tell by the markings that it's two years old. The mane and tail have been braided and groomed. And this is a western riding saddle on its back."

"Why, Peter, that's *perfect!*" Mrs. Hooping-Koff exclaimed.

"And this is the rider that goes with Peter's horse," Patty Perfect said. "The crease in his cowboy hat shows that he's worn it forever. And I've carved buckskin chaps over his legs. And, as you can see, the boots I gave him are European leather."

"Perfect," Mrs. Hooping-Koff said, nodding.

Patty slid the rider onto the saddle of her brother's horse. He fit perfectly, and they pushed their sculpture to the center of the table so everyone could see it.

"If you'd like to see more of our clay work," Peter said, "you can visit our exhibit at the Youth Art Museum. Our sculptures will be on display until next September."

"The exhibit is titled *Perfect Works in Clay*," Patty added.

Peter turned to Mrs. Hooping-Koff. "Do we get extra credit for having a museum exhibit? We also have a website."

Before our teacher had a chance to answer, Rob Slob called out, "I'm finished! Check mine out!"

He pointed to a lumpy thing on the table in front of him.

"What *is* that?" Mrs. Hooping-Koff asked.

Rob Slob grinned. "It's an armpit." He started to raise it off the table.

"No! Please don't raise your arm!" I cried.

"Please! Please keep your arm down!" Mrs. Hooping-Koff pleaded.

"No! No armpit! *Don't open your armpit!*" Adam Bomb shouted.

But the alarmed cries around the table didn't stop Rob.

He raised his clay model above his head. And that meant his own real armpit was open.

And the stench swept over the room like a tsunami of stink. In seconds, we were all choking, gagging, and holding our noses and our breath.

Mrs. Hooping-Koff stumbled to the corner of the room and had dry heaves.

Kids began to cry.

The clay sculptures on the table wilted under the weight of the aroma.

"Hey—someone in here stinks!" Rob exclaimed.

I told you, the lucky guy can't smell his own smell.

My eyes were watering. I couldn't breathe. The odor came in waves, pushing me off my stool.

Just before I hit the floor, I heard Adam Bomb choke out, "We have to do something about Rob."

"I ... have ... a plan," Brainy Janey whimpered.

And then she began choking and gagging, and we didn't get to hear the rest of what she had to say.

SEVENTEEN

Brainy Janey here. If I may . . .

After dinner that night, we had a meeting about what to do with Rob Slob. We sat around the dining room table and talked. Rob was at the table, too. But he had no idea we were talking about *him*.

Wacky Jackie had a good idea. "We fill a barrel with honey and lower him into it," Jackie said. "He would come out smelling as sweet as honey."

"Why don't we fill the barrel with horse manure?" Cranky Frankie said. "He would *still* come out smelling better than he does now."

Rob Slob laughed. "Ha ha. That's funny. Who are we talking about?"

"You don't know him," I said, thinking quickly.

I turned to the others. "There are two problems with

Jackie's plan. One, we don't have a barrel. And two, we don't have any honey."

"We could use the bathtub," Babbling Brooke said. "And fill it with water."

"I think that's called a *bath*!" Handy Sandy said.

"A bath! Brilliant idea!" I exclaimed.

"We have a bathtub?" Rob Slob asked.

"I think it's somewhere in the bathroom," Wacky Jackie said.

I nodded and turned to Rob. "Rob, how do you feel about baths?" I asked.

He grinned. "Bath? What's a bath?"

"We'll show you," I said. "Would you like a hot bath or a cold bath?"

"Yes," he answered.

"What kind of soap do you like?"

"I don't remember," Rob said.

"How about shampoo?" I asked.

"How about it?" he replied.

We all stared at him in silence. This was a big moment in our house. Rob Slob was willing to take a bath. This would improve our lives forever!

"Can we give you a bath right now?" I asked. My heart was pounding with excitement.

"Sure," Rob answered. "Why wait?"

Suddenly, I had a hunch. "Rob, stand up," I said.

He pushed his chair back from the table and climbed to his feet.

"Turn around," I said. "Turn around and take your T-shirt off."

"Whoa. Wait," Babbling Brooke cried. "Are you sure you want him to do this right here? The smell—"

"Rob, pull off your T-shirt," I insisted.

"Okay, Janey."

Rob Slob obediently lifted his shirt and tugged it off over his head.

"Just as I suspected," I said.

I reached over and pulled a live snapping turtle off Rob's back.

"Rob, look at this. You have so much vegetation on your skin, you had a turtle *living on your back*!"

I held the turtle up for everyone to see. Some gasped. Others made gulping noises.

"Didn't you feel it back there?" I asked.

Rob shrugged. "I guess it itched a little," he said.

"I hate to think what's living in his *pants*!" Cranky Frankie said.

EIGHTEEN

Luke Puke uttered a sick groan and climbed to his feet. "Where's the best place to throw up my dinner?" he said.

"At the Perfects' house next door!" Wacky Jackie joked.

"No time for that," I said and turned to Handy Sandy. "Sandy, start the water going in the tub."

"I'll need pliers for that," Sandy said. "Someone stole the knobs off the faucet."

"Just get it going," I said. "Make the water real deep. We want Rob to stay in there a long time."

"Not too hot," Rob said. "I have sensitive skin." He scratched his arm and several ants fell off and scurried away.

I gave Rob a gentle shove. "Go get undressed. Adam and Luke will escort you."

"Don't worry, I'll keep him underwater for a long time," Luke said. "He needs to soak the stink off."

"But he has to br-breathe!" Nervous Rex said.

"He can breathe *after* his bath," Luke said.

"Find him some soap," I told Sandy.

Rob looked thoughtful. "I saw a photo of soap once," he said.

A few minutes later, I heard the water running in the tub in the bathroom across the hall. Then I saw Rob Slob, in a ragged brown bathrobe, trotting to the bathroom. Adam Bomb and Luke Puke were behind him, holding their noses.

We all listened until we heard the splash of Rob plopping into the tub. It was a seriously awesome sound. It meant the air was going to smell a lot sweeter.

Everyone—and I mean *everyone*—was smiling. Except for Cranky Frankie. He had the usual scowl on his face.

"Frankie, what's your problem?" I asked. "Rob is finally taking a bath."

"A bath isn't going to help," he muttered. "Rob smells from the *inside*!"

"That's not n-nice!" Nervous Rex exclaimed.

Cranky Frankie turned to him. "Haven't you noticed? I'm not nice. But I'm *honest*."

We were all listening to the sounds of Rob splashing

around in the tub when Adam Bomb poked his head out of the bathroom.

"How's it going?" I asked.

"It's going okay," Adam reported. "But as soon as Rob got into the tub, the water turned a yucky green. Algae, I think."

"Just make sure he soaps himself up," I said.

"Anyone care for some Mulch Chunks?" Junkfood John asked. He held up a bag. "Very crunchy. And they really do taste like mulch."

No one took John up on his offer.

Then the doorbell rang.

I blinked in surprise, then glanced at the clock over the mantel: it read 8:30.

Who would come to see us at this time of night?

I pulled open the door—and let out a cry.

NINETEEN

Adam Bomb again. I'll take things from here...

Brainy Janey jumped back from the door. I saw the startled look on her face, and a second later, I knew why.

Parker and Penny Perfect stepped into the house. They were dressed perfectly. Their clothes didn't have a single wrinkle, and their shoes were brilliantly polished.

As Janey stepped back, the Perfects immediately began looking around the room, studying each of our faces.

"Sorry to stop by so late," Mrs. Perfect said. "But we brought your parents a little treat."

That's when I saw the little white cake box in her hand. "Does your mother like baloney cake?" Penny Perfect asked.

"Uh . . . yes . . . no," Brainy Janey answered. "She . . . uh . . . doesn't like baloney, but she likes cake."

"My wife makes a perfect baloney cake," Parker Perfect said. "She uses only organically grown baloney. That's how you know it's good."

The Perfects had smiles pasted on their faces. But we knew why they had come to visit, and it didn't have anything to do with cake . . . or baloney.

They wanted to prove we didn't have parents.

That way they could get us out of the house, and out of their neighborhood.

Mrs. Perfect raised the cake box in front of her and dangled it. "Can I give this to your mother?" she asked.

"Well . . ." I could see that Brainy Janey was stumped. So I stepped up to the Perfects. "You see . . ." I started. "Mom isn't home right now."

"Oh, that's too bad," Parker Perfect said. "Where is she?"

"She's on her way home," I said.

"But she was in an accident," Wacky Jackie chimed in.

The Perfects gasped.

"An accident? Oh my, what happened?" Mr. Perfect asked.

"She drove into a puddle," Jackie said.

"A puddle?" Mrs. Perfect repeated. "What kind of accident is *that*?"

Jackie blinked. "Did I say puddle? I meant *poodle*."

Mr. Perfect squinted at her. "Your mother ran into a poodle?"

"But which was it?" his wife asked. "A poodle or a puddle?"

"Both," Jackie said. "That's why she's late. The poodle was in the puddle."

Penny Perfect shook her head. "I don't understand. She didn't see the poodle in the puddle?"

"It was a mud puddle," Jackie said.

"The poodle had to piddle," Babbling Brooke chimed in.

"Yes, it had to piddle in the puddle," Jackie agreed.

The Perfects stared at each other for a moment, then turned back to us.

"I don't understand at all," Mrs. Perfect said. "The poodle had to piddle? In the puddle?"

"It was standing in the middle," Brooke said.

"And your mother drove into the poodle with her car?" Mr. Perfect asked.

"Mom doesn't have a car," I said.

"She was on her bike," Jackie said. "And she pedaled into the poodle in the puddle."

Mrs. Perfect blinked several times. "I'm ... not getting this," she stammered.

"It's simple," Brooke replied. "We wanted to play ping-pong. So Mom went out to buy us paddles. But she pedaled into the puddle and hit the poodle, and dropped the paddles in the puddle."

"And then the poodle had to piddle," Jackie added. "Mom called and said it piddled on the paddles."

"And that's why Mom isn't here," I said.

Mr. Perfect shut his eyes for a minute. "I'm beginning to understand this," he said. He opened his eyes and narrowed them at me. "You don't have a mother—or a father—do you? You're living here by yourselves. And you're making up all this nonsense to fool us!"

"You mean there's no poodle?" his wife asked.

"There's no poodle and no puddle and no parents, either," Parker Perfect said. "You are trying to get us to leave by making up some crazy story. You think that will get rid of us?"

The Perfects were smarter than I'd thought. I think they were beginning to catch on.

"Let me be honest with you," I said. (That's what I always say when I'm about to tell a lie.) "Our mom is *dying* to meet you. And when we tell her she missed your visit, she'll be very disappointed."

As I reached for the box, they both stared, studying me. They were trying to decide if I was a good liar or a *really* good liar.

But before they could say anything, there was a commotion coming from the hall. Clumping footsteps. And a cough.

We all turned to see Rob Slob walk into the room. He wore his ragged brown bathrobe, the belt tied tightly over his stomach. And his hair was still wet from the bath. "Hey, what's up?" he called out.

"**EEEUUUW.** What's that *smell*?" Mr. Perfect cried, and pinched his fingers over his nose.

Mrs. Perfect groaned. "**OHHH,** that horrible odor. It smells like *burned skunk*!"

All around the room, everyone groaned and covered their noses.

Parker Perfect started to gag, and pressed a hand over his mouth.

"The smell . . ." his wife uttered. "It's making my eyes water. I . . . I'm going to be sick!"

Covering their mouths and noses, the Perfects spun around—and bolted out the front door. We could see them running full speed across the lawn.

"What's their problem?" Rob Slob asked.

Handy Sandy came up behind him. "Good news and bad news," Sandy said.

Choking and gagging, we all turned to her.

"The good news is, Rob took a bath," Sandy said. "The bad news is, a bath makes him smell a lot *worse!*"

"Hey, look!" Junkfood John cried. "The Perfects left their baloney cake. Anyone want to split it with me?"

BRAINY JANEY'S HISTORY QUIZ

Here is a quiz I took in school last week. Of course, I aced every question. Mrs. Hooping-Koff said my answers were the most amazing she'd ever seen.

How many of these can you answer?

My answers are on the next page.

QUESTIONS

1. Who was the first president of the United States?

2. Finish this famous line the young George Washington said after he was caught chopping down a cherry tree: "I cannot ____"

3. How do you spell Massachusetts?

4. The pilgrims arrived in a new land. They brought very few supplies. What was the main thing they ate?

5. Who was the brilliant colonial inventor who flew a kite to experiment with electricity? Ben ____

6. Who was Paul Revere?

7. Can you describe the first Thanksgiving?

8. Who were the Redcoats?

9. What did the Declaration of Independence say?

10. If you lived in colonial times, what job would you like to have?

ANSWERS

1. A New England colonist named Marcus Absent declared himself the first president in 1722. At that time, there was no United States. It was later discovered there was no Marcus Absent. He was completely made up.

2. "I cannot tell a lie. I want to kill all cherry trees because I hate the pits."

3. M-A-S-S-A-C-H-U-S-E-T-T-S.

4. They mainly ate food.

5. I believe his name was Ben Dover. People used to laugh at his name, especially since his best friend was Stan Dupp.

6. Paul Revere is the answer to Question #6 in this quiz.

7. Yes. The pilgrims decided to hold it on Thanksgiving Day. They didn't have turkeys in those days, so they ate maize, which is another word for something or other.

8. Ben Franklin invented the first red coat. Before then, coats were in black and white. All people were in black and white, too, for many centuries, until color TV was invented.

9. Sorry. I haven't read the Declaration of Independence. I'm waiting for the movie.

10. King.

TWENTY

I'm Babbling Brooke. It's my turn to tell this story now...

I was standing next to Junkfood John in line at the school cafeteria, when he got into a fight with one of the lunch helpers.

"Fritos is *definitely* a vegetable!" John insisted.

"First I've ever heard of it," the woman replied without changing her expression.

She had a long white apron over her clothes and wore a net over her short brown hair. In her hand was a big scoop, and she was dishing out macaroni and cheese to anyone who wanted some.

A white name tag pinned to her apron read: ANNIE.

"Potato chips come from potatoes, right?" John asked.

Annie nodded.

"Well," John reasoned, "Fritos come from Frito trees. They're harvested like any other vegetable."

Annie sneered at him. "Guess you've done a lot of research," she said.

John nodded. "Did you know pretzels are considered a fruit," he asked. "Like Froot Loops. And I'm pretty sure popcorn comes from the leaves of cucumber bushes."

"Thanks for all that *useful* information," Annie said, tapping her big scoop on the counter. "Can I ask you a question, young man? You came here from what planet?"

Junkfood John didn't get a chance to answer.

Because that's when a food fight broke out.

And that's when I began to worry about Cranky Frankie.

TWENTY-ONE

The boys in our house call me Babbling Brooke, I guess because I like to talk a lot. I know they think of me as this flaky rah-rah cheerleader type.

But I'm also the worrier in our family.

I mean, *someone* has to worry about us kids. Here we are, on our own, with no mom or dad. We have to be kids *and* grown-ups at the same time. And we're not exactly like the other kids!

Brainy Janey is a serious brainiac. She's so smart, you can never tell *what* she's thinking! And since she's too busy thinking all the time, I kind of see it as *my* job to look after everyone.

And I instantly became worried about Cranky Frankie when the food fight broke out. He just sat there and didn't even bother to jump in.

It all began when Junkfood John smashed half a cantaloupe into Luke Puke's face.

Why did he do it, you ask?

Don't ask me.

Luke Puke let out a shrill cry. "Food fight!" he screamed. "Food fight!"

Some kids didn't even look up from their macaroni. We have a food fight around 12:30 every day.

It's actually a school sport.

Peter and Patty Perfect once asked if they could get extra credit for tossing food at other kids. I think Mrs. Hooping-Koff said okay. She loves the Perfects.

Luke Puke then poured a bowl of tomato soup over Junkfood John's head. The thick, lumpy soup ran down his cheeks. I had to laugh. It looked pretty funny.

Kids jumped up from their tables, eager to join in. The cafeteria food isn't worth eating. But it sure is good enough to throw at other people.

I didn't move fast enough, and Wacky Jackie smushed an open peanut-butter sandwich into my face. And guess what? I jumped up and began cheering:

"FOOD FIGHT! FOOD FIGHT!

"WE'VE GOT THE VEGGIES! WE'VE GOT THE CARBS!

"WE'VE GOT THE—YIIIKES!"

I couldn't finish because someone slid a vat of spaghetti down my back.

Screams broke out as a whole tray of creamed spinach went flying off the food table. It landed with a **SPLAT** on top of a bunch of eighth graders. It oozed down them like lava on a volcano.

Someone heaved a huge glob of banana pudding at Junk-food John. It splattered on his chest and stuck there. John looked down, scooped some up with his hands, and jammed it into his mouth.

I ducked as two chicken legs whirred over my head. They flew under the next table and hit Nervous Rex, who was hiding down there.

The screams, the crack of plates, and the **PLOP** of flying food filled the cafeteria.

Suddenly, a shrill whistle burst through the deafening racket. It was a long whistle, followed by another long whistle.

The room began to quiet down as Coach Swettypants blew his whistle. Food stopped flying. And the shouts faded to groans and murmurs.

Everyone turned toward Coach, who blew his whistle until he was red in the face. Junkfood John kept eating pudding off the front of his pants.

"Hope you enjoyed your lunch, everyone!" Swettypants boomed. "Now wipe yourselves down and get to class!"

TWENTY-TWO

As we all started to parade toward the cafeteria doors, Coach stopped Adam Bomb and pulled him aside. "You've got a good arm, Adam," he said. "I saw the way you heaved that ham across the room."

"I've been working out a little," Adam said.

"Maybe you'd like to join our football team," Coach Swettypants said. "We need someone who can throw a good ham."

Our team, the Smellville Stinkworts, hasn't won a game. Ever. But we are very good losers.

We've been the All-State Number One Losing Team for five years in a row. That's something to be proud of.

You can always tell the guys on the football team in our school. They're the ones with big casts on their arms and legs, and they walk around with crutches.

"Think about it," Swettypants said to Adam Bomb. Then he let him join the others hurrying to class.

I had my eyes on Cranky Frankie the whole time. He still sat in his seat, sipping a box of Frooty Pelican Juice with a straw. His eyes were down, and his whole body was slumped in the low cafeteria seat.

I motioned to Handy Sandy. "Look," I said, pointing.

She turned and studied Frankie. "What's the problem, Brooke?" she asked. "Frankie always drinks Frooty Pelican Juice. He likes the taste of pelican."

"You don't understand," I said. "Look at him. He hasn't moved."

"So?"

"He didn't throw any food, Sandy," I said. "You know what Frankie can do with potato salad. And you've seen him send tubs of mustard flying clear across the lunchroom."

Her mouth dropped open. "You mean—"

"He didn't join in the food fight—his favorite sport," I whispered. "He just sat there, looking sad and depressed."

"Uh oh," Handy Sandy said, shaking her head. "We've got a problem."

TWENTY-THREE

Hey, remember me? Your old friend, Adam Bomb. It's my turn again to tell the story...

That night after dinner, Ptooey the Parrot and I were having one of our insult battles.

I leaned over the squawking bird and said, "I'll feed your feathers to the cat!"

"Ptooey! You don't have a cat!" the bird shot back.

"I'll buy one. And you can change your name to Cat Food!"

"Ptooey! Ptooey! Change your name to Litter Box! Squawwwk!" And just like that the bird lifted its leg and plopped something onto my shoulder.

"GAAACK!" I cried and stepped back. Sometimes that feather-faced idiot makes me so mad, I think I'm going to explode.

"Hey, give it a rest," Handy Sandy called out. "I thought we were having a house meeting."

"Ptooey! Ptooey! Come back here, Litter Box. I've got another present for you! Squawwwwk!"

PLOP!

I turned and trudged into the living room, muttering to myself and wiping my shoulder with my hand.

Everyone was sprawled around the room, still burping from our dinner—meatballs with a side of meatballs on top of meatballs in a meatball sauce.

Awesome.

There's a meatball restaurant around the corner from us. And it's *the* place to go, especially if you like meatballs.

They don't have anything else. Well . . . they *do* have dessert. But . . . dessert is coconut meatball pie. And not even Junkfood John will eat that.

"We need to talk about Cranky Frankie," I said.

Nervous Rex gazed around the room. "Where is he?" Rex asked. "Is he s-sick? Is he lost? Did he break something? Does he need a doctor? Is he in trouble? Did he leave? Is he g-gone forever?"

"Don't be so nervous, Rex," I said. "Frankie's in his room. He said he's too sad and depressed to come out."

Junkfood John's eyes lit up. "Did he finish his meat-balls?" he asked.

"He didn't have an appetite," I said.

"Can I have them then?"

"Not now, John—" I started.

Junkfood John held up a bowl. "I have pickled eel sauce from a week ago, if anyone is interested." He raised the bowl to his mouth and poured the sauce down his throat.

"We have to get serious about Frankie," I said.

"Yes, he's totally depressed," Brooke chimed in. "He didn't throw anything in the food fight today at lunch.

And he didn't say anything cranky at dinner, either."

"He just sat there," I said, "with a blank look on his face. His eyes were dull, and he stared into space. His mouth hung open, and he never even raised his head."

"So what's different about him?" Wacky Jackie exclaimed, then laughed at her own joke.

"It isn't funny," Brooke scolded her. "He's too sad and depressed to be cranky. We have to cheer him up."

"Ptooey! I'll cheer him up!" the parrot squawked from across the room. He lifted one leg. **"Bring him here! I've got a present for him!"**

"Shut your yap, Ptooey!" Luke Puke yelled.

"You shut your yap!"

"No, *you* shut your yap!"

"No, you shut your yap!"

"No, *you* shut your yap!"

"No, you shut your yap!"

"No, *you* shut your yap!"

"No, you shut your yap!"

"No, *you* shut your yap!"

"No, you shut your yap!"

"No, *you* shut your yap!"

"No, you shut your yap!"

"No, *you* shut your yap!"

"No, *you* shut your yap!"

"No, *you* shut your yap!"

"No, *you* shut your yap!"

"No, *you* shut your yap!"

"No, *you* shut your yap!"

"No, *you* shut your yap!"

"No, *you* shut your yap!"

"No, *you* shut your yap!"

"No, *you* shut your yap!"

"No, *you* shut your yap!"

"No, *you!*"

"No, *you!*"

"*You!*"

"*You!*"

"Both of you—SHUT UP!" I screamed.

We all knew that Luke and the parrot had the same IQ. But why couldn't Luke realize he was never going to win an argument with Ptooey?

"Sit down, Luke," I said.

"**Sit down, Luke,**" the parrot squawked.

"No, *you* sit down!" Luke screamed.

"**No, *you* sit down!**"

"No, *you* sit down!"

"**No, *you* sit down!**"

104

"No, *you* sit down!"

"No, *you* sit down!"

"No, *you* sit down!"

"No, *you* sit down!"

"No, *you* sit down!"

"No, *you* sit down!"

"No, *you* sit down!"

"No, *you* sit down!"

"No, *you* sit down!"

"No, *you*!"

"No, *you!*"

"*You!*"

"*You!*"

I couldn't take it any longer. My head was vibrating, buzzing, about to explode. There's a reason my name is Adam Bomb. My head really *was* about to blow up all over the living room.

And it's very messy, trust me. Not to mention the headache afterward.

I had to do something.

I ran to Ptooey, stuffed him into his cage, and pulled the cover down over it.

Then I darted to Luke's bedroom, yanked the blanket off his bed, ran back into the room, and threw the blanket over Luke.

Finally, peace and quiet.

"*Now* can we talk about Frankie?" I asked.

"We have to think hard," Brainy Janey said. "We have to cheer him up so he'll be his old cranky self again."

Janey had been thinking so hard all day, she had steam pouring out of both ears and her eyebrows formed the word TILT.

"What can we do?" she asked. "Any one have any ideas?"

TWENTY-FOUR

I have an idea," Babbling Brooke said, and jumped to her feet. "I wrote a new cheer to *cheer* Frankie up. Get it? Watch me. See if you think it will work."

She clapped her hands, leaped into the air, and began her cheer...

"CHEER UP! CHEER UP! CHEER ALLLL THE WAYYYY UP!

"UP UP UP. UP WITH THE CHEER.

"YOU CAN BE CHEERFUL! GIVE US AN EARFUL!

"DA DAA DAA DUH DA DA DA."

The cheer ended in a split. I heard Brooke's knees crack. She probably broke something.

Brainy Janey helped Brooke up from the floor.

As she limped to the couch she said, "It isn't quite finished. I'm still working on the last line. But ... what do you think?"

"Needs work," Wacky Jackie said. "Like maybe a new beginning, middle, and end. Hahaha."

Brooke smiled. "Does that mean you like it?"

"What else can we do to cheer Frankie up?" I asked, changing the subject.

"Maybe we could tickle him," Wacky Jackie said. "That always works for me."

"He doesn't like to be touched," I said.

"We could tickle him with a feather," Jackie replied. She turned to the parrot cage. "And I know where we can get the feather."

"Awwwk. Ptooey!" the bird cried, underneath his cage cover. **"Come over here. I'll use your face for a pincushion!"**

I groaned. "Can't anyone shut him up?"

"Can't anyone shut *him* up?" the bird squawked. **"Come closer. Awwwk. I'll spit between your eyebrows!"**

I groaned again. "I know what would cheer Frankie up. A nice bowl of parrot soup!"

"How about some pickled eel sauce?" Junkfood John suggested and raised his bowl. "I still have a little left."

"That won't cheer Frankie up," I said. "He's so sad and depressed, he isn't hungry, remember?"

"I have an idea," Brainy Janey said.

The room instantly became silent.

Whenever Brainy Janey has an idea, it's always smart and good and seriously awesome. So we all gazed at Janey, waiting for her to speak.

"How about a balloon?" she said.

TWENTY-FIVE

Huh?" I gasped. "That's your brilliant idea? A balloon?"

Janey nodded. "But not just any old balloon. A *red* balloon."

"Poor Janey," I said. "You've been hanging out with Wacky Jackie too much. She drained your brain."

"I don't get it," Jackie said. "Is that a compliment? I think that's a compliment, right?"

"I think a balloon is a good idea," Janey said. "You know, Frankie once told me that no one had ever given him a balloon."

I squinted at her. "He said that?"

She nodded again. "Frankie said that when he was very little, he went to a carnival. And a man came by carrying a huge bunch of helium balloons on strings. Frankie wanted one so bad, but the man walked right past him. All these years later, no one has ever given Frankie a balloon. He's been cranky ever since."

Nervous Rex held a tissue to his face. "S-stop," he said. "You're making me cry. That's the saddest thing I ever heard." His shoulders heaved up and down as he sobbed.

"Ptooey! Awwk. _You're_ the saddest thing I ever saw!" Ptooey called. **"You want a reason to cry? Come over here. I'll peck your arteries out! Awwk."**

"Shut your yap," Luke Puke shouted at the parrot from under his blanket. "I'll pluck you like a bad guitar!"

"_You_ shut your yap!"

"No, _you_ shut your yap!"

*"**You** shut your gap!"*

"No, *you* shut your yap!"

*"**You** shut your gap!"*

"No, *you* shut your yap!"

*"**You!**"*

"You!"

"Well . . . let's try the balloon idea," I said. "Who wants to go to the store and buy a red balloon? They have them at the Smellville Party Store."

Handy Sandy raised her hand. "I'll go get one," she said, and started to the front door.

"Hurry back," I said. "I hate to see Cranky Frankie so sad."

"Back in a jiffy," Sandy replied as the door slammed behind her.

Three days later, Sandy returned with a red balloon.

"What happened?" I asked. "Where have you been?"

TWENTY-SIX

Brainy Janey again. I think it's best if I continue the story from here...

Cranky Frankie was so depressed, he stayed in his room for three whole days. I told him he was missing school and he said, "No. I don't miss it at all."

I tried to get him to insult me or yell. But he was still too sad to be cranky.

Finally, three days later, Handy Sandy came walking in carrying a red helium balloon on a string.

"What happened?" Adam Bomb asked Sandy. "Where have you been?"

Sandy shrugged. "It's kind of a long story." As she tied the string to the back of her chair, she sat down and started to tell us the story.

"I went to the Smellville Party Store for a red balloon,"

Sandy started, "but the owner sent me to the balloon store down the street. I got to the balloon store, but they were out of balloons."

"So what did you do?" I asked Sandy.

"I waited while they drove to the next town to get more balloons."

"And?" I asked impatiently.

"They came back a few hours later with about a dozen balloons. But none of them were red. They had blue and green and pink and yellow and gray and brown and black and rainbow and chartreuse. But no red."

"So what did you do?" I asked.

Sandy sighed. "What could I do? I waited for them to go back to the next town and get a red balloon. Later that night they came back with a red balloon. I was so happy and asked them to blow it up. But it turned out their helium tank was empty."

"They had no helium?" Adam Bomb asked.

Sandy nodded. "No helium."

"So what happened?" I asked.

"They had to fly to the next state to refill the helium tank," Sandy said. "I waited for them. But it took a day before they returned with a filled tank."

"So they filled the red balloon with helium?" I said.

Sandy nodded again. "Yeah, they filled it. But then they realized they didn't have any string."

I groaned. "You're kidding. They were out of string?"

"Yes," Sandy answered.

"So what did you do?"

"Well . . . the string store was closed. So I had to wait overnight until they opened again. The next morning, I bought a string and tied it to the red balloon.

"So I was all set and headed home. But then something bad happened . . ."

"Something bad?" Adam asked.

She nodded. "I was so excited, I accidentally let go of the string. And the red balloon floated away."

"So what did you do?" Adam demanded.

"I went back to the balloon store for another one. But they had to drive to the next town again, and they came back the next day with another red balloon."

She grinned. "And now here I am. I brought it home as fast as I could."

"Well, let's go give it to Frankie," I said. "I can't wait to see his face. This is going to cheer him up instantly."

Handy Sandy untied the string from her chair. The red balloon bobbed above her head.

She carried it carefully up the stairs to Frankie's room. Everyone followed as we stopped in the hall and crowded around his bedroom door. I knocked.

"Come in," Frankie said evenly.

I opened the door and we stepped inside. "We have a present for you," I said.

Frankie raised his head and gazed at the balloon.

"Here." Sandy handed him the red balloon.

We waited. And waited.

Then Frankie started to cry. And his cries became loud sobs.

"Huh? What's wrong?" I asked him.

"I wanted a *blue* balloon!" Frankie said.

JONNY PANTSFALLDOWN

Favorite TV superhero of Wacky Jackie and Junkfood John
Episode 342

Zip your fly, everyone! Snap to attention! And keep your belt buckled tight for ADVENTURE! It's time for another thrilling episode of JONNY PANTSFALLDOWN, told by me, the world's greatest sidekick—THE MIGHTY HAIRBALL!

"I will never let you down!" That's what Johnny Pantsfall-down promised the good people of Pupick Falls.

And he always keeps his word.

Every night after dinner, Jonny puts on his cape, his mask, and his Pants of Steel. Then, side by side with me—the Mighty Hairball—he fights crime and terrifies criminals with his famous battle cry:

"YODEL-AY-EEE-OOOO!"

As our story begins, Jonny is at the stove, frying an egg for his Power Dinner. I am sitting at the kitchen table, blowing my nose into my stylish Mighty Hairball handkerchief.

"Did you have dinner?" Jonny asked.

I nodded. "I had an ear of corn," I said. "It's all I was in the mood for."

Jonny flipped his egg over with a spatula. "You know, Hairball, you're supposed to shuck the corn first before you eat it."

"You're joking," I said. "You mean open it up first?"

"Yes," Jonny replied. "You're not supposed to eat the leaves."

I burped into my hand. "I never knew that, Jonny. I'll try to remember next time. The leaves always stick in my throat. And so do the corn cobs."

I'm really lucky to be the sidekick of Jonny Pantsfalldown. I learn something new every day. Why, just last week, Jonny taught me how to tie the laces on my boots. And ever since, I haven't been falling down as much.

Jonny flipped his egg again and it sizzled in the pan.

"Funny thing about eggs," Jonny said. "You can cook them sunny-side up. You can cook them over, or bottoms up. But you can't cook them sideways."

"I'm sure science is working on that," I said.

Jonny is so brilliant. He's not only an expert on catching criminals, he's also an expert on eggs.

I watched him slide the egg onto his plate beside a slice of toast and walk toward the table.

But the sad fact is, Jonny never got to eat that egg.

The life of a superhero is unpredictable.

Before Jonny could slide even a sliver of egg down his throat, he was off on one of the most dangerous and thrilling adventures of his life!

JONNY PANTSFALLDOWN CONTINUED...

"No time for dinner!" Jonny cried. **"I'm getting a police signal from my pants! We have a crime to stop!"**

Jonny's Pants of Steel are on alert twenty-three hours a day. (The other hour, they are in the wash!)

He turned to me. "Mighty Hairball, we've got to get to Lake Sickening. I hope we're not too late!"

"The lake?" I cried. "Is someone in trouble there?"

"No," Jonny answered, lacing up his high-heeled boots—the boots that make him look almost as tall as other superheroes. "Someone is *stealing* the lake!"

I slapped the sides of my face with both hands. "Oh no! Lake Sickening is the most beautiful spot in all of Pupick Falls. Despite its odor."

"It's Big Bootus again! My archenemy!" Johnny exclaimed. "Big Bootus is trying to steal the lake and put it in his own backyard!"

"He can't get away with that!" I cried, pulling down the ear flaps on my battle helmet.

"Not with Jonny Pantsfalldown on duty," Jonny said. He then raised his head and shouted his famous battle cry:

"YODEL-AY-EEE-OOOO!"

"Did you bring that new belt buckle?" Jonny asked. "The buckle with a double lock for keeping my pants up?"

"Shoot, I forgot it," I said.

I may be the world's best sidekick, but I'm not perfect.

"No problem," Jonny said. "I'll worry about that later. Now let's go rescue the lake!"

We jumped out the window and took off flying into the night sky. The moon was full and the stars were bright, and I could hear my stomach gurgling.

You guessed it. I'm afraid of heights.

Jonny's Pants of Steel ruffled in the wind as we flew side by side. I shut my eyes and pretended I was down on the ground. I get terribly airsick, you know.

"It's a big lake. How are we going to find Big Bootus?" I asked.

"He's easy to find," Jonny replied. "He has the biggest bootus in town."

A few minutes later, Lake Sickening was below us, shimmering under the bright moonlight. And there on the shore stood Big Bootus, gazing up at us as we landed.

"Well, well, it's the Mighty Hairball!" he sneered. "I see you brought your puppy dog with you to play!"

"I don't own a puppy dog!" Jonny Pantsfalldown boomed.

"I meant it as a joke," Bootus replied. "It was kind of an insult."

"I don't get jokes!" Jonny shot back. "I'm too busy protecting the people of Pupick Falls to waste time deciphering your jokes!"

Suddenly I felt muddy water pour into my boots. I had accidentally stepped into the lake.

I tried to back up, but both boots were now filled with water. I dropped to my knees and my pants got all wet, too.

Oh wow. I struggled to my feet and saw that my cape was soaked.

"You'll never get away with this, Big Bootus!" Jonny shouted. "Lake Sickening belongs to the *people*!"

Big Bootus grinned. "It's mine now! I'm taking it home, Jonny."

"But—how?" Jonny demanded.

JONNY PANTSFALLDOWN CONTINUED...

"Do you see these ten thousand water glasses?" Big
Bootus said. He motioned to the glasses lined up
along the shore.*

"What do you plan to do with those?" Jonny asked.

"I've filled them all up with water! I've already got half
the lake, and I'm taking the glasses home in my truck and
pouring them into my backyard!"

Jonny turned to me. "This is a tough one. He has a pretty
good plan, Hairball. What do you think we can do to stop him?"

"Maybe you could punch him," I said. It's a sidekick's job
to always be thinking and planning and plotting.

"I can't allow you to steal Lake Sickening,"
Jonny said. Fists raised, he then let out his battle cry:

"YODEL-AY-EEE-OOOO!"

Big Bootus laughed. "What are you going to do, Jonny?"

"Punch you really hard in the stomach," Jonny told him.

But Big Bootus laughed again. "You'll have to catch me first!" And with that he spun around and took off, running along the shore, his big bootus bobbing behind him as he ran.

Jonny took a deep breath and rocketed after Bootus. "I won't have our lake stolen on my watch!" he shouted.

Big Bootus was too big to run too fast. I watched as Jonny came up behind him.

And then: **"WHOOOOOAAA!"** Jonny's pants fell down.

He tripped and stumbled forward—falling face-first into what was left of Lake Sickening.

"Noooo! Mighty Hairball—help me!" Jonny cried. "My Pants of Steel are pulling me down, down to the bottom. I'm going to drown!"

I ran over to him. "I can't help!" I told him. "I don't know how to swim. They don't have a pool at Sidekick School."

Jonny splashed and thrashed and kicked and squirmed. Finally, he just rolled out of the lake (after all, there was only two inches of water left).

By the time we turned around, Big Bootus had loaded all the water glasses into his truck. We stood there watching as he drove away with the lake.

Jonny sighed. "If only I had that belt buckle with the two locks," he said.

"I'll try to remember it next time," I told him. "The Mighty Hairball never forgets . . . twice!"

Jonny waved his fist at the back of Big Bootus's truck as it rolled away. "I'll get you next time!" he yelled. "Or my name isn't Jonny Pantsfalldown!"

That's our thrilling adventure for today, boys and girls. Until next time, this is the Mighty Hairball saying: "Keep your pants up—and reach for the stars!"

TWENTY-SEVEN

Okay, Adam Bomb here again. I tried to get everyone to turn off the TV so we could discuss our parent problem. But another episode of *Jonny Pantsfalldown* was about to start.

It was one of our favorites. The one where Jonny puts his Pants of Steel on backward, *and he walks into himself*! It's an awesome episode, so no one would turn it off.

And then it was dinnertime, and I was starting to get hungry.

You might wonder how the ten of us feed ourselves without any parents in the house. Well, it isn't that hard.

Some nights we sneak into other people's houses and eat their dinner before they sit down. The Fayce-Wart family lives next door to the Perfects. They leave their kitchen window open a lot, and it's easy to sneak out big helpings of their dinner when they're not in the kitchen.

Most nights, though, we make our own food.

Handy Sandy is an awesome cook. Junkfood John is good, too.

Sandy's best dishes are cold spaghetti out of a can and microwave popcorn. John has been into vegetables lately. His favorite is candy corn.

My favorite dinner is a can of vanilla icing and tortilla chips.

Last night, however, we had a problem. Babbling Brooke and Brainy Janey were enjoying a salad. But as they dug in, they found a lot of feathers in it.

It turns out Ptooey had been in the kitchen before dinnertime. The girls finished their salads, but they choked on the feathers and even ate the strange white dressing they didn't remember putting on.

We never all sit down together to eat at the same time. For one thing, we don't have a table big enough for all of us. We usually just go into the kitchen and grab something when we feel like it.

Tonight, I was watching *Jonny Pantsfalldown* with everyone else. Junkfood John and Wacky Jackie came out of the kitchen with big smiles on their faces and orange sauce dripping on their chins.

"I'm stuffed," Jackie said, patting her stomach.

"Awesome dinner," John said to Handy Sandy. "Were you the one who made it?"

Sandy turned away from the TV. "Made what?"

"That big bag of dinner we just ate," John said.

"Oh, wow." Sandy shook her head. "I meant to take that bag out to the back. That wasn't dinner. It was last week's garbage."

"Tasty," John said, wiping his chin.

TWENTY-EIGHT

I think I should explain that garbage is very important here in Smellville.

For one thing, the metal garbage can was invented in this town. Before that, people used paper garbage cans, and they always got soggy and fell apart.

One fun fact: The man who invented the metal garbage can thought he was inventing a garbage *pail*. He had no idea he was inventing a garbage *can*, not a pail.

That's one of the "interesting" things they taught us in fourth grade, the year all students study the history of garbage in Smellville.

You see, Smellville is a tourist town because of our garbage. The Tomb of the Unknown Sanitation Worker stands in the middle of Waste Matter Park.

People come from miles around to gawk at the twenty-foot-tall bronze statue in front of the tomb—a sanitation worker in a stained uniform, with an enormous garbage can hoisted over his shoulder.

It's an awesome statue. People are so inspired by it, they bring their garbage and leave it there in tribute.

No one even knows who the fallen sanitation worker is. The plaque on his tomb just says that he gave his life to rescue a garbage bag that was floating out to sea.

At the bottom of the plaque are the words: *So long, sucker.*

I believe that's Latin for: *Rest in Peace.*

Now, you may be wondering why all of Smellville Middle School is here at the Tomb of the Unknown Sanitation Worker.

Relax, I'm going to tell you in the next chapter.

(Hint: It has something to do with garbage.)

TWENTY-NINE

So here I am at the Tomb of the Unknown Sanitation Worker with everyone else from my school.

That's because it's Middle School Garbage Day.

Each year we come here to celebrate our unknown hero. And every kid brings some garbage from home to enter in the big contest.

That's right. Our principal, Mr. Grunt, will award the Best Garbage of the Year trophy to one lucky winner. I told you, garbage is important to us here in Smellville. Everyone wants to win the first-prize trophy.

I felt bad, though. We didn't have much garbage to enter in the contest this year. That's because Wacky Jackie and Junkfood John *ate* most of it.

"I'm so tense. Do you think we have a chance?" Nervous Rex asked me.

I checked the bags in front of me. They were leaky and some orange lumpy stuff was dripping out from the bottoms. "It smells totally putrid," I told Rex. "I think it smells bad enough to win the trophy."

Rex held his nose. "That's not our garbage that stinks so bad. It's Rob Slob."

"You can't even smell garbage when Rob is standing next to it," Cranky Frankie added.

I turned to Rob. A whiff of powerful odor made me sneeze a few times.

I noticed he had green-and-blue mold growing on his jeans. "Rob, do you ever clean your jeans?" I asked.

Rob squinted at me. "You're supposed to *clean* them?"

I nodded. "When mold starts to grow on your jeans, you probably should wash them."

"No one told me I had to," he said.

"You should wash your shirt, too," I said. "It's all mossy and has leaves growing on it."

"I'm not wearing a shirt," Rob said.

I had to turn away. His breath was melting my buttons.

Peter and Patty Perfect walked by me. They were carrying their garbage in a pale blue shopping bag from Tiffany's, the jewelry store.

"Our garbage doesn't smell," Patty said to me.

"Yeah. *Your* garbage smells like garbage," Peter said, holding his perfect nose in the air. "We spray our garbage with perfume before we bring it here. Then we Febreze it. Then we perfume it again. That's why Patty and I always win."

"Maybe we should spray Rob Slob," Cranky Frankie whispered to me.

I started to say something, but Principal Grunt waved for everyone to be quiet.

Babbling Brooke trotted up to the front of the statue. Brooke had been practicing her garbage cheer for days. She was totally stoked to cheer in front of the whole school. And we were all hoping she didn't mess up.

"GIVE ME A G!" she shouted.

And everyone shouted back: "G!"

"GIVE ME AN A!" Brooke cried.

"A!"

"GIVE ME AN R!"

"R!"

"GIVE ME AN A!"

"A!"

"GIVE ME A G!"

"G!"

"GIVE ME AN E!"

"E!"

"WHAT DOES THAT SPELL?" Brooke asked.

"Garage!" everyone yelled back.

Oh, wow. Too bad. She left out the B.

Brooke did two cartwheels to finish. The first cartwheel was awesome. In the middle of the second cartwheel . . . she landed on her face.

Two kids helped carry her away as Principal Grunt stepped up to the podium.

That isn't his real name. We actually don't know his real name because he only grunts, and no one can understand a word he says. So we just call him Principal Grunt, and he doesn't seem to mind.

At the podium, Principal Grunt tapped the microphone a few times. Then he brought his face close to it and said:

"*Grunt grunt gruntgruntgrunt grunt grunt gruntgrunt. Grunt grunt? Grunt rrrrrunnnt rrrrrunnnt grunt grunt?* Yes! *Grunt grunt grunt!* Agree?"

Everyone mumbled and murmured. We didn't know how else to answer.

"*Grunt grunt rrrrrunnnnt gruntgruntgrunt,*" he continued. And then a smile crossed his face as he said: "*Grunt grunt* garbage *gruntgruntgrunt grunt grunt gruntgrunt.*"

Principal Grunt held up the first prize trophy. Big and silver, it gleamed under the morning sunlight.

I held my breath. Was it possible? After all, our garbage *was* the best we'd ever had.

Could we win the trophy this year?

"Grunt grunt!" Principal Grunt shouted. "*Grunt grunt grunt.* And the *grunt* winner is . . ."

THIRTY

Everyone grew quiet. The whole school, all 250 of us. We were standing in front of the statue of the Unknown Sanitation Worker. Of course, even though they call us Garbage Pail Kids, we aren't into garbage. But we *are* into trophies.

Who doesn't want a shiny silver trophy to brag about?

We all want to be winners. It doesn't matter that the contest smelled to high heaven.

And so we all stood there in silence, leaning toward Principal Grunt at the podium. Waiting . . .

"The winner *grunt* is . . ." he repeated.

But he didn't get to make his announcement.

Everyone gasped and cried out as a big dog came bounding across the grass. The dog's ears were flat against its head and its tail wagged furiously as it galloped toward the podium.

Nervous Rex bumped me from behind. "H-hey—isn't that *our* dog? How did Pooper get out of the house?"

I shielded my eyes from the sun with one hand so I could see better.

Yes! It *was* Pooper!

And to prove beyond a doubt that it was our dog, he stopped in front of Principal Grunt, squatted—and began to poop.

Kids laughed and shouted.

Principal Grunt's face turned red as a tomato and he shook the trophy angrily in the air.

"Pooper is ruining the whole award c-ceremony!" Nervous Rex cried.

I laughed. "I think he's *improving* it!"

Rex began to tremble. "If Grunt finds out he's *our* dog, he'll find a way to punish us."

"Wow! Pooper must have had a *big* breakfast!" I cried. "Look at him go!"

Two teachers ran out to chase Pooper away. But our dog *never* moves until he has finished his business.

At the side of the podium, Babbling Brooke began to jump up and down and cheer.

"GO, POOPER!

"GO, POOPER!

"YOU'RE SUPER!

"BETTER GET A SCOOPER!

"GO, POOPER!"

Cranky Frankie shook his head. "She'll cheer for *anything*," he muttered.

"I sure hope she doesn't try another cartwheel," Nervous Rex said. "If she falls facedown . . ."

Pooper finally finished. And then trotted away to a standing ovation.

His head was high, and his tail was wagging. I wondered if he knew that everyone was cheering for him.

I could see Principal Grunt at the side of the podium. He was bent over, puking his guts out into the trophy cup.

Coach Swettypants stepped up to the microphone. "Did anyone bring a shovel?" he shouted.

Of *course* no one brought a shovel. Why would they?

"Well . . . be careful, people!" he said. "Walk around it! Walk around it!"

Good advice.

Swettypants turned and watched Principal Grunt throwing up into the silver trophy. Then he turned back to the microphone. "We'll get that trophy cleaned later," he announced. "Don't worry. It will be as good as new!"

Everyone grew quiet again.

"Principal Grunt has a very sensitive nose," Coach said. "So he's a little under the weather right now. That leaves it to me to announce the Smellville Middle School winner of the Garbage of the Year Award."

Coach held up a small card with the winning name on it. "And the winner is . . ."

THIRTY-ONE

Can you feel the suspense?

"And the winner is . . ." Coach Swettypants shouted into the microphone. "The Perfect Twins—Peter and Patty!"

"Not again!" I moaned.

A few kids clapped as Peter and Patty walked side by side up to the platform.

I had my fingers crossed and held my breath. But they carefully stepped around Pooper's contribution to the ceremony.

The twins moved behind the podium and slapped about ten or twelve high fives with each other. Then they turned to the crowd with smiles that were actually wider than their faces!

"My perfect sister and I are so happy to bring home the trophy again!" Peter Perfect exclaimed.

"Well, we'll be happy to bring it home *after* it's cleaned," his sister added.

"We try to be perfect in everything," Peter said. "Even garbage."

"You may not know this," Patty said. "But we *gift wrap* our garbage before we take it out to the curb and place it in the garbage can. That makes it nicer for our garbage collector."

"That's just how perfect we are!" Peter declared. "We *care* about our garbage."

"We even donate tons of garbage every year to the homeless!" Patty said. "We know they can't afford garbage of their own. So we do what we can for them! It's the least we can do."

A few kids clapped at that. But not many.

The Perfect twins walked off, trying to keep their big grins from flying off their faces. Those kids sure do like to win.

"We should start saving up our garbage for next year," Cranky Frankie said to me.

"Good idea," I said.

Patty and Peter stepped up to us. "Sorry your garbage didn't win," Peter said.

"Sorry your trophy is filled with puke," I replied.

"Your backyard should win a *garbage prize*," Patty Perfect said. "You have a *mountain* of trash back there."

"We're just waiting for the garbage cans to get full before we take them out," I said.

"You don't have any *garbage cans*," she replied. "You just have *garbage*."

"How do you know?" I demanded. "Have you been snooping in our backyard?"

Patty Perfect had her nose in the air. "No, but our parents have," she said.

"Our parents say your backyard is a health hazard," Parker said. "They say your garbage is three feet deep."

"They *measured it*?" I asked.

The twins both nodded. "Yes, they measured it," Patty answered. "They are not spies. But they do keep a notebook of information about you and your friends. My parents say you've ruined the neighborhood. And they're going to get you out. They're going to make the neighborhood *perfect*."

"Perfect? *Without us?*" I cried.

"How else could it be perfect?" Peter said.

Patty sneered at us some more. "Our parents are going to pay you a surprise visit tonight. And when they see you have no parents, they're going to report you and have you all sent away."

I swallowed. "They're paying us a surprise visit?"

"Yes," Patty said. "They're going to surprise you at seven o'clock tonight."

"And when they see you have no mom or dad," Peter added, "they will report you to . . . whoever you report things to."

I stared at them with my mouth hanging open. I didn't know what to say.

A surprise visit tonight at seven. That's not good. Not good at all. But what could we do?

THIRTY-TWO

After school, we had a meeting to decide how to get ready for the surprise visit by Mr. and Mrs. Perfect. Once they see we have no mother or father tonight, we are doomed.

As I explained to everyone what would happen to us, I could feel the anger and fear building up inside me. I gripped my head in both hands. It felt like I could explode at any minute.

"I—I feel sick," Nervous Rex stammered. He turned to Wacky Jackie and stuck out his wrist. "Would you take my pulse? I think it's beating too f-fast."

Jackie wrapped her fingers around Rex's wrist and counted silently to herself. "You don't have a pulse," she said finally.

"Oh, thank goodness!" Rex cried. "I was worried that I did!"

"I'm so upset, I feel sick, too," Luke Puke said, and pressed a hand over his mouth. **"ULLLLLLP."** He then jumped up and went running to the bathroom.

"He's no help in an emergency," Cranky Frankie said.

Babbling Brooke leaped up from her seat on the couch. "I have an idea. What if I do a cheer for the Perfects? It might put them in a really good mood and make them forget why they came here."

She bent down low, then jumped into the air.

"GO, PERFECTS! GO, PERFECTS!

"UH . . . UH . . ."

Brooke turned to me. "What rhymes with *perfect*?"

"Maybe we should forget that idea," I said. "You know, Brooke, doing a cheer won't solve *every* problem."

She squinted at me. "It won't?"

"I have an idea," Wacky Jackie said. "It's simple. We run to the store, and we buy an apron."

"An apron?" I asked.

She nodded. "Yea, we buy an apron that says WORLD'S BEST MOM on it. And we leave it in the kitchen."

"Brilliant! Brilliant!" a shrill voice rasped. It was Ptooey behind us on his parrot perch. **"Brilliant for a bird brain!"**

"You shut up!" Wacky Jackie shouted.

"No, *you* shut up!"

"No, *you* shut up!"

"No, *you* shut up!"

"No, *you* shut up!"

"No, *you* shut up!"

"No, *you* shut up!"

"No, *you* shut up!"

"No, *you* shut up!"

"No, *you* shut up!"

"*Stop!*" I screamed, holding the sides of my head. "We don't have time for arguments."

"Bird seed for brains!" Ptooey squawked.

"You shut up!" Wacky Jackie shouted.

"No, *you* shut up!"

"Hold on, everyone!" Handy Sandy spoke up. She came walking into the room, carrying something between her hands. "Who is the handy one here, guys? That's right, you're looking at her!"

Sandy grinned and held up the object she was carrying. "No worries. Problem solved!"

THIRTY-THREE

We all jumped up and gathered around Handy Sandy.

"Stand back!" she cried. "I'm dangerous!"

I pointed to the thing she was carrying. "What is that?"

"It's a *welcome* mat," she said, raising it in front of her.

We all scratched our heads. None of us had ever seen one before. "What does it do?" Wacky Jackie asked.

"You put it outside your front door," Sandy explained. "People step on it and wipe their feet before they come into the house."

"Why?" Rob Slob asked.

I shook my head. "How does that solve our Perfect problem, Sandy?"

She grinned. "Easy." She stretched out the brown, fuzzy mat. It said WELCOME in black letters in the center.

"It looks like a normal welcome mat," she said. "But I've improved it. I put a bear trap inside."

I squinted at it. "A bear trap?"

Sandy nodded. "Let's say Mr. and Mrs. Perfect come up to the door. Mr. Perfect steps on the welcome mat—and it *snaps*! The trap slams shut around his ankle, and he falls to the ground screaming."

"Sounds good to me," Cranky Frankie said.

"Imagine Parker Perfect on the ground screaming his head off," Sandy continued. "And they're trying to pull the trap open, but they can't. So Penny Perfect calls 911. An ambulance arrives and takes them *both* away."

"I like it," Cranky Frankie said. "Simple but painful."

"And they never find out that we don't have any parents," Brooke said.

"Bird seed for brains!" Ptooey squawked.

"You shut up!" Wacky Jackie shouted.

"No, you shut up!"

I scratched my head. "Sandy, you tried the electric doorbell shock trick on them—remember? And it didn't work at all."

"That's because I forgot to turn it on. And it was electric," she explained. "This is a simple metal trap. There's nothing to plug in or turn on. It *can't* fail."

I frowned. "Hmmm, are you sure?"

"I'll show you," Sandy said, and spread the mat out on the floor. "Are you watching?"

She stepped onto the mat with her right foot.

SNAAAP!

"OWWWWWWWWWW!"

The trap snapped shut around her ankle.

Sandy dropped to the floor and grabbed her ankle, howling her head off in pain.

"Bird seed for brains!" Ptooey squawked.

"You shut up!" Wacky Jackie shouted.

"No, you shut up!"

Sandy thrashed around on the floor, tugging at the mat wrapped around her ankle.

"OWWWWWWWW!"

She uttered another howl—

—when the doorbell rang.

We all gasped. The room grew silent except for Sandy's cries and howls.

"Is it Parker and Penny Perfect?" I asked. "Did they come early?"

"OWWWWWWW!"

Rolling on the floor in agony, Sandy uttered another shrill howl.

I had to step over her to get to the front door.

When I pulled it open—I stared at a woman wearing a dress with biker boots. She had spiky purple hair and squinty eyes. Leaning on a wooden cane, she scowled at me.

"Don't just stand there, ferret face. Aren't you going to let me in?" she barked. "I'm your mother."

THIRTY-FOUR

I gasped and nearly swallowed my tongue. I could feel my heart start to flutter in my chest. "You—*you're my real mother*?" I choked out.

"Of course not, you dum-diddy!" she exclaimed.

She raised her cane and shoved me aside with it. Then she stepped into the living room, her tiny eyes darting from side to side.

"Hey, donkey brains, say hi to your ma!" she shouted.

Everyone just stared at her.

Pooper made a whimpering sound. He usually races to greet every visitor. But he stayed in his corner, his big brown eyes watching the woman carefully.

"**Awwk.**" Behind us, Ptooey raised one leg. "**Come over here, Ma. I got a present for you!**"

The woman turned to the birdcage. "A parrot! I love parrots. I like them slow-cooked with fingerling potatoes. They taste just like chicken! Ha ha ha!"

Ptooey lowered his leg and got very silent.

The woman puckered her red-lipsticky lips and made a sound like **SMACK SMACK SMACK.** "Who wants a big kiss from Mama?"

Before anyone could reply, Brainy Janey came walking through the front door, lugging a large suitcase. "Brainy Janey to the rescue!" she declared. "I got us a mom."

"Don't applaud . . . just throw money!" the woman cried. Then she cackled at her own joke.

She motioned to her suitcase. "Just take that to my bedroom. I'll make myself at home."

Janey dragged the bulging suitcase to the back.

"You're staying?" I blurted out.

"I'm staying—and so is my friend!" she rasped, raising the cane above her head. "Meet my friend—the Enforcer!"

"But—" I started.

She swung the cane hard and smacked me in the back with it.

WHAAAAPPPPP!

Howling in pain, I staggered halfway across the room.

Then she turned to Luke Puke on the couch. "Hey, cluck-cluck—get your feet off the coffee table."

"That's not a coffee table," Luke said. "It's Junkfood John."

John lifted his head. "Nice to meet you," he said without getting up.

She sniffed the air. "What's that disgusting odor? Do you keep rotting meat in here?"

"No . . . it's Rob Slob," Wacky Jackie said.

"Well, tell him to take a bath!"

"*Nooo!*" everyone shouted.

"A bath just makes him smell much worse!" Jackie explained.

The woman turned to Rob, who was wiping his runny nose with the sleeve of his shirt. "You sleep in the garage from now on!" she said.

"But . . . we don't have a garage!" Rob protested.

"Then *pretend!*" she cried.

Janey walked back into the room and put a hand on the woman's shoulder. "We have our mom. We're all set for the Perfects. After tonight, they won't bother us again."

"You can call me Mama!" the woman rasped. "Or Ma or Mom. Just don't call me late for supper! Ha ha ha!"

Mama swung her cane and smacked Nervous Rex in the knees with it.

He uttered a sharp cry of pain.

"Hey, cluck-cluck—why didn't you laugh at my joke?" Mama demanded.

Rex started to shake. "Because I'm a little afraid of you," he murmured. "You—you're making me nervous."

"Your *face* is making me nervous!" she exclaimed.

Luke Puke jumped up and went running to the bathroom, his hand over his mouth.

"Janey, where did you find her?" I asked.

"I rented her," she replied.

"I'm a Rent-a-Mom," the woman said. "You've heard of us, haven't you?"

"Yes, of course," I lied. I didn't want to be smacked by the cane again.

I came close and whispered in Janey's ear: "She's a little weird."

"That's why she was half price!" Janey whispered back.

"Awwwk. Give me a kiss, Mama!" Ptooey squawked. **"I'll bite your beak!"**

"Somebody toss that bird in the oven for me," Mama ordered. "I'll have it for dinner with lettuce and tomato on ciabatta bread!"

THIRTY-FIVE

Cranky Frankie here. I have to continue the story because Adam Bomb's head blew up. And it wasn't pretty.

It's kind of a long story. With an *explosive* ending.

But I'll get to that later.

For now, we were all staring at our new mom. She sure was tough, swinging her cane around and calling us names.

But, I thought, maybe she'll fool the Perfects when they show up. And then we'll be done with our Perfect problem for good.

The kids in this house are all gross, lame-brained, worthless slobs. But they are my friends. No, change that. They are my *family*. And I didn't want to see my family scattered.

Babbling Brooke has a picture on her bedroom wall. It says: HOME SWEET HOME. I don't know about the *sweet* part. But it *is* home. For all of us. And we really wanted to keep it that way.

"Stand up, you dum-diddies!" Mama shouted, waving her cane. "We have a lot of work to get this place looking good for the Perfects. She then gazed down at the floor. "Has any of you cluck-clucks swept the floor lately?"

"There's too much junk and stuff on it," Handy Sandy answered. "We can't *find* the floor."

"Stay away from that squishy part over there," Nervous Rex said, pointing to the corner. "It might be quicksand."

Mama smacked her cane down on the floor. "Somebody bring out the broom!"

"We don't have a broom," Adam Bomb said.

"Okay, then, bring out a mop!"

Adam shook his head. "We don't have a mop."

"How about a DustBuster?"

"What's *that*?"

"Okay," Mama said. "Bring out a cleaning brush."

"We don't have one of those, either."

"How about a rake?"

"No," Adam said, "no rake."

"A shovel?"

"No shovel."

"How about a sponge?"

"We had a sponge once, but Pooper ate it."

Mama tore at her purple hair with both hands. "Does anyone have a *toothbrush* we can use?"

Silence.

"How about a toothpick?"

Silence.

"What about a fork? A screwdriver? A butter knife? Tweezers?"

Adam Bomb suddenly grabbed the sides of his head.

"Stop! Please—stop! I—I can't take any more of this!" he cried. "We don't have any cleaning tools. No one ever told us we'd have to clean up!"

His eyes spun crazily as he gripped his head. His face went from red to purple.

"Can't take it! Can't take it!" he repeated.

There was a low **BUZZ.** It became a rumbling sound— like an earthquake in a movie.

Adam's eyes bulged. His face darkened to a deep magenta.

And then . . .

BAAAAARRRRRRROOOOOOOOOMMMMMM!

His head blew up.

Adam's head just exploded all over.

A shocked silence fell over the living room.

We all gaped in horror, gasping and choking, staring at a headless Adam as he slumped to the floor.

Finally, Mama broke the silence. "Okay, okay," she said. "Forget about cleaning up. Some other time, maybe."

THIRTY-SIX

Luke Puke and I carried Adam to his room and dropped him onto his bed.

We've seen him explode many times before. Adam has a very *explosive* personality.

I'll admit watching a friend's head blow up can be pretty upsetting. But once you've seen it a bunch of times, it's no big deal.

When Luke and I returned to the living room, everyone was discussing dinner.

"We need to show Mr. and Mrs. Perfect that we're a normal family," Brainy Janey said. "When they arrive, we need to crowd around the table, and have a family dinner cooked by Mama. That will send the Perfects on their way."

I squinted at Mama. "Can you cook?"

Mama nodded. "I was a cannibal for ten years when I was younger. I can cook *anything*."

Janey grinned. "See, Mama is going to save the day."

Mama rubbed her hands together. "You diddy-wads are in for a treat," she said. "Lead me to the kitchen and bring me your biggest frying pan."

Janey took Mama's elbow and led her into the kitchen. I heard pots and pans clanging and banging in there.

"Okay," Mama called. "Bring me that fat parrot so I can cut its head off! Who wants to help me pull off its feathers?"

"I will!" Wacky Jackie volunteered. She jumped up from her chair and started to the birdcage.

"Awk. You shut up!" Ptooey squawked.

"No, *you* shut up!"

"No, *you* shut up!"

"No, *you* shut up!"

"No, *you* shut up!"

"No, *you* shut up!"

"No, *you* shut up!"

"No, *you* shut up!"

"Wait! Stop!" Nervous Rex cried. "We can't eat the parrot."

"Why not?" Wacky Jackie demanded.

Rex held his belly. "Every time I eat parrot, it upsets my stomach."

"Ptooey! How about a bite?" the parrot squawked at Mama. **"Come over here. I'll give you a bite you won't forget!"**

Mama shook her head. "Okay, I'll make something else for you cluck-clucks."

She turned and looked out the window at our backyard. "I see you have vegetables growing in the garden. I'll pick some of them and make a stew."

"Uh . . . those aren't vegetables," Janey told her. "It's garbage that has taken root."

Mama stepped into the dining room. "Let me think . . . let me think of something I can cook. I think—"

She stopped with a short cry. And her eyes bulged as she stared at our dining room table.

She pointed with a trembling finger. "Is that . . . is that a dead cow on the dining room table?"

Everyone turned to the table.

"No," I said. "It's Junkfood John. Sometimes he falls asleep there."

I poked John in the stomach. "Wake up. Come on, get up. We need the table. It's almost dinnertime."

John groaned and rolled off the table and onto the floor.

"Hey, everyone—" Babbling Brooke called from the middle of the living room.

We all turned to her.

"Whose turn is it to walk Pooper?" she shouted.

Handy Sandy raised her hand. "It's my turn," she said.

"Well, good news. You don't have to walk him," Brooke said. "He just made a big pile on the floor."

Mama's little eyes went wide as she stared at the floor. "Does anyone ever clean up after Pooper when he does his business in the house?"

"Almost always," Sandy said.

And that's when the front doorbell rang.

The Perfects were here.

A STRETCHING EXERCISE FROM COACH SWETTYPANTS

Listen up, people.

This story is getting tense.

Here's a simple stretching exercise you can do to help you stay relaxed through the next part of the book. It's easy. And you don't need any special equipment, either. You can do it wherever you are, indoors or outdoors or even without doors.

1. Let's start at the top. Move your head around and around in a circle until you hear a soft cracking sound in your neck.

2. Ignore the pain and keep rotating your head, listening for the CRACK CRACK CRACK of your neck muscles loosening up.

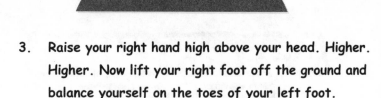

3. Raise your right hand high above your head. Higher. Higher. Now lift your right foot off the ground and balance yourself on the toes of your left foot.

4. Now reverse. Raise your left hand and your left foot and balance on your right toes. Listen up, people. If you fall over, don't get discouraged. Try balancing from a sitting position.

5. Now here's the real stretch. Bring your left leg up and entwine it under your right arm.

6. Bring your left arm under your right leg and hold it till you feel the stretch behind your knees.

7. Fold both hands under your knees and tuck your legs over your arms.

8. Hey, I seem to be stuck here. I can't seem to untangle my arms and legs.

9. Can anyone help me? I'm in a lot of pain here, and I just heard something snap in my back.

10. I really do need some assistance. Is anyone out there? Can anyone help get my legs free so I can crawl to the nurse's office?

11. Anyone?

THIRTY-SEVEN

Cranky Frankie here. As I was saying . . .

You could feel the tension in the room. It suddenly felt as if the air had frozen, and some of us kids started to shiver. Nervous Rex bent over and tucked his head between his knees. Sort of like an ostrich hiding in the sand.

Luke Puke made an **ULP** sound and went running to the bathroom.

"Don't panic, you dum-dum doo-doos!" Mama shouted. "I know how to handle these people. After all, *I'm* perfect, too!"

Handy Sandy held up her welcome mat with the bear trap hidden inside. "Is it too late to use this?"

"Put that thing away. We don't need it," Mama said. "Go on, get it out of here."

Sandy took a few steps toward her room and—

SNAAAAAAAPPP!

"OWWWWWWW!"

She fell to the floor, howling in pain.

Mama waved her away with her cane. With her leg trapped inside the welcome mat, Sandy staggered out of sight.

The doorbell rang again and Mama turned back to us.

"Open the door, nit-nits! And stop panicking. We got this. First, I'm going to drive them crazy. Then I'm going to make it so they can't *wait* to leave!"

"I know she can do it," Brainy Janey said. "Renting Mama was the smartest thing I ever did."

"True that!" Mama said, slapping Janey on the back so hard her bubblegum came flying out. "Now, keep them busy while I change." Then she ran to the back of the house.

Junkfood John pulled open the front door.

Mr. and Mrs. Perfect grinned at him. "Surprise!" they cried in unison. "We thought we'd pay you a *surprise visit.*"

"You're early," John said. "Did you bring us treats again?" He started to drool. The word *treats* always gets him drooling.

"No treats. May we come in?"

The Perfects didn't wait for an answer. They pushed past John and strode into the living room. As they stood at the entrance gazing around the room, they inspected us.

"I love that brown vase on the rug," Mrs. Perfect said. "It's so natural looking. Where did you get it?"

"Pooper made it," I said.

She smiled at me. "Someone here is very talented."

"Awk! Ptooey!" the parrot squawked from his perch. **"Come over here, and I'll make something for _you_!"**

"Are your parents home?" Parker Perfect asked. "We're so eager to meet them."

"Mama is home," Janey told them. "She'll be right out."

The Perfects blinked. "She is?"

They couldn't hide their surprise. They had come to trap us, to find us without any parents. But we were prepared.

I held my breath. A lot of questions flew through my mind.

Could our Rent-a-Mom really fool them?

Could she convince the Perfects she was our mother?

And what about our dinner?

THIRTY-EIGHT

Uh... how is your mother doing?" Penny Perfect asked.

"The last time we were here, you told us she had all her teeth pulled."

"Oh," Janey said. "Well... they put them all back in."

The Perfects blinked again. "That's good news," Penny said.

"She'll be happy to show you her teeth," Wacky Jackie said. "They came from a horse. They're totally awesome."

Mr. Perfect gasped. "Your mother's teeth came from a horse?"

Jackie nodded. "Her old teeth were too small. She kept swallowing them."

The Perfects exchanged a long glance. I could see this wasn't going well. They were starting to get suspicious.

"Horse teeth?" Mr. Perfect asked.

Jackie nodded. "But you should see how Mama eats carrots now. She's a champ."

Mrs. Perfect turned to me. "Is your mother really home?"

"She told us she was home," I said.

Mr. Perfect frowned at me. "When?"

"When she was home," I said.

"She told you she was home when she was home?"

"She said she'd be home," I said.

"Hold on," Penny Perfect said. "Where was she when she told you she'd be home?"

"Home!" I answered.

"Here I am!" a voice called from the doorway.

Everyone turned as Mama strolled into the room.

Her cane tap-tapped the floor in front of her as she stepped up to greet the Perfects. She had dressed up as an old-fashioned housewife in a flowery skirt and a frilly white blouse. And she had a yellow apron tied around her waist.

"You must be the P-P-Perfects!" she gushed, and sprayed the P-P-Ps all over Parker Perfect.

He wiped his face with a handkerchief.

"So nice to meet you. And what is your name?" Penny Perfect asked.

Mama raised a hand behind her ear, as if she couldn't hear. "Pardon?"

"Your name," Penny Perfect repeated. "What should we call you?"

Again, Mama raised her hand behind her ear. "Pardon?"

"*What is your name?*" Mr. Perfect shouted.

"Pardon."

"YOUR NAME! YOUR NAME!" he cried.

"You don't have to shout," Mama said. "My name is Pardon. Papa named me Pardon."

"What a strange name," Mrs. Perfect said.

Mama put her hand behind her ear. "Pardon?"

"Yes, Pardon," Mrs. Perfect repeated. "Very strange."

Again, Mama placed her hand behind her ear. "Pardon?"

"IT'S A STRANGE NAME!" Mr. Perfect screamed.

"You don't have to shout!" Mama scolded him again. "Papa was sitting there in jail. Mama thought he was a goner. But, sure enough, the pardon came through from the governor. So he came home and named me Pardon."

"How interesting. What did your father do for a living?" Penny Perfect asked.

Her hand went behind her ear. "Pardon?" And then Mama went, "*Hic, hic . . .*"

"Your father," Mr. Perfect said. "What did he do for a living?"

"Pardon? *Hic, hic.*"

"WHAT DID YOUR FATHER DO FOR A LIVING?" Peter Perfect screamed.

"You don't have to shout," Mama said. "*Hic, hic.*"

"Why is she doing that?" Babbling Brooke whispered to me.

"I think she's trying to be totally annoying," I whispered back.

"It's working," Brooke whispered.

Mr. Perfect took a deep breath and curled and uncurled his fists. Both of their faces were red. I could see that Mama was driving them crazy.

"We just wondered what your father did for a living," Mr. Perfect repeated, gritting his teeth.

"He was a murderer," Mama said. "Can I offer you some cookies?

THIRTY-NINE

"I'm so happy to have visitors," Mama told the Perfects. "Come, sit down on the couch. *Hic, hic.*"

"That isn't the couch," I said. "That's Junkfood John."

"What adorable children you have," Mrs. Perfect lied. She had a tight grin plastered to her perfect face. "Do I detect a slight accent? Where are you from?"

Mama cupped both ears with her hands. "Pardon? *Hic, hic.*"

"Do you have hiccups?" Mrs. Perfect asked.

Mama shook her head. "*Hic, hic.* No."

"Where are you from?" Mrs. Perfect repeated.

"Pardon? *Hic, hic.*"

"Oh, never mind!" Mrs. Perfect snapped.

"Mars," Mama said.

"Is that the way people speak in . . . on . . . Mars?" Mr. Perfect asked.

Mama cupped her ear. "Pardon? *Hic, hic.*"

Mr. Perfect uttered a cry of frustration.

Mama was driving the Perfects insane. *Perfectly* insane. She was driving *me* insane, too!

Parker Perfect turned to Wacky Jackie. "Let me ask you. Where did you all come from?"

Jackie cupped a hand behind her ear. "Pardon? *Hic, hic.*"

Beside her, Handy Sandy cupped her ear. "Pardon? *Hic, hic.*"

The *hic*s traveled quickly around the room.

"*Hic, hic.*"

"*Hic, hic.*"

The Perfects covered their ears with their hands. They had their mouths wide open, like they both wanted to scream.

Mrs. Perfect turned to me. "So all you kids belong to her?" she asked.

I cupped my ear. "Pardon? *Hic, hic.*"

She muttered something under her breath. Then she turned back to Mama. "So all these kids are yours?" she demanded.

"Awk! Ptooey! Pardon? *Hic, hic,*" Ptooey squawked.

"They are *all* mine. *Hic, hic,*" Mama answered. "They're adopted. From a dog pound."

The Perfects gasped. "A *dog pound*?"

Mama thought hard. "No, maybe it wasn't a dog pound. They didn't have any dogs. They only had kids. *Hic, hic.*"

"How many?" Parker Perfect asked. "How many kids *do* you have?"

Mama rubbed her chin. "Well . . . *hic, hic.* There were ten. But last time I looked, there were only nine."

Patty Perfect uttered a shocked cry. "You lost one?"

Mama shrugged. "It happens."

FORTY

Brainy Janey here. I was bursting with pride. When I rented Mama and brought her home, I had no idea she would be so *perfectly* annoying.

I hoped she would be able to get rid of the Perfects. And she was doing her job *really* well—almost too well.

I think everyone in the room wanted to scream. And tear their hair out and bang their foreheads against the wall and jab pencils into their eyeballs and plug up their ears and twist their heads off.

Mama was having that effect on *everyone*.

Even Pooper hid in a corner and covered his ears—and eyes—with his paws.

When Mama went into a full-blown *hic-hic-hic* fit, spitting and *hic*ing all over the Perfects, I could see our neighbors move quickly toward the front door.

In a few seconds, they would be gone, and we would all be safe. But they suddenly stopped.

"Hey, we're stuck!" Penny Perfect cried.

We looked down and saw their shoes were stuck in some kind of thick yellow stuff clumped on the floor.

They struggled to free themselves. "My shoes are totally caught. What is this gunk?" Parker Perfect cried.

Mama shrugged. "*Hic, hic.* It wasn't there yesterday. It must have grown overnight."

Penny Perfect gasped. "You mean it's *alive*?"

Mama nodded. "Pardon? *Hic, hic.*"

"You have *got* to clean this house," Penny Perfect said. "It's dangerous. And it's a health hazard."

"Pardon? *Hic, hic.*"

"I SAID, IT'S A HEALTH HAZARD!" Penny Perfect shrieked. She tugged one foot out of its shoe, which stayed stuck in the yellow goo.

"Ptooey! Welcome to Smellville!" the parrot squawked.

"*Hic, hic.* I know, I should do some light dusting."

"Light dusting?" Parker Perfect cried. "You need to burn the house down and start over."

Mama nodded. "Yes. *Hic, hic.* Maybe a good cleaning. And a little bug spray."

The Perfects nodded.

"That's why I have the kids all packed up," Mama said.

Mrs. Perfect scrunched up her face. "Packed up?"

Mama nodded. "Yes, their bags are all packed. Don't you worry. *Hic, hic.*"

"Why are they packed up?" both Perfects said at once.

"Why? To move into *your* house, of course," Mama said.

"*Hic, hic!*" Now even the Perfects started to *hic*.

"Isn't that why you came by? To let me know they can move in with you while I clean up?" Mama asked.

"NO! NO WAY!" Parker Perfect cried. "*HIC, HIC.*"

"*HIC, HIC!* NO WAY! NO WAY!" Penny screamed.

Mama turned to us kids. "The Perfects are such good neighbors. You kiddos will be on your best behavior, right?"

We all cupped our hands behind our ears and yelled, "Pardon? *Hic, hic.*"

"NO WAY! NOT HAPPENING!"

"NO! FORGET IT! NO!"

The Perfects' bare feet slapped the floor as they ran to the front door.

"You're all just a bunch of . . . Garbage Pail Kids!" Mrs. Perfect screamed.

A few seconds later, the door slammed behind them.

And like that, they were gone.

We all sat there staring at their two pairs of shoes still stuck in the gooey floor.

There was silence for a few seconds—we were all in shock.

Then everyone leaped to their feet, cheering and shouting and laughing and hugging and slapping high fives and doing fist bumps and victory dances.

Babbling Brooke broke into a cheer:

"THEY'RE GONE! THEY'RE GONE!

"YAAAY . . .

"What rhymes with gone?"

Then everyone huddled around Mama, who took a

deep bow. "Don't thank me. Just throw money," she said. She said that more than a few times.

I patted her on the back. "You were awesome! The Perfects won't bother us again for a long time."

"Great job!" Handy Sandy cried and gave Mama a hug. "You're the *best!*"

Everyone cheered again.

"We can't thank you enough," I said. "I'll pay you the rest of what we owe you, and then you can go home."

Mama grabbed my arm. "Huh? Go home?"

I nodded. "Yes, your job is over. You were terrific. Now you can go home."

A thin smile spread across her face. "Good news, dum-dums. I've decided to stay."

We all gasped in surprise.

"I like it here," Mama said. "I'm going to stay for a long time. Maybe I can get you boneheaded baloney-faces to shape up."

"But—but—but—" I sputtered.

She slapped me on the back with her cane. "You're not a motorboat. Stop the putt-putt-putt!"

Then she turned to Handy Sandy and Babbling Brooke. "Hey, cluck-clucks—go get your things out of the bedroom. That's *my* room now."

FORTY-ONE

Junkfood John here, continuing the story.

Luke Puke, Nervous Rex, Rob Slob, and I stayed up late to celebrate. The others were exhausted from all the tension and excitement and went to bed. Even Mama.

I ate two bags of tortilla chips and a couple frozen pizzas to tide me over till breakfast. Rob Slob pulled some crumbs from his hair and ate them. I have no idea what they were.

Nervous Rex paced back and forth, his hands clasped behind his back.

"Rex, what's your problem?" Luke Puke asked.

Rex shook his head. "I'm w-worried. I think Mama is going to be trouble. We've always done fine without any parents. I just know we're going to be s-sorry."

Rob Slob burped four or five times. Then he said, "Sorry? Why will we be sorry?"

And then we heard a deep rumble of thunder.

No, not thunder.

Rex stopped walking back and forth. Luke jumped to his feet. Rob stopped burping.

Another deep rumble shook the walls.

"What is that noise?" Luke asked.

The four of us tiptoed to the back hall. The lights were out, but we could see that Mama's bedroom door was open. Another roar made the floor tremble beneath us. And I thought I heard the ceiling crack.

"She—she's snoring!" Rex exclaimed.

I dropped the bag of chocolate-covered cotton-candy chips I had in my hand. "Yeah, she's snoring, all right."

"RRRRRHONNNNNK RRRRRRHHHHHHNNNNNNK!"

Behind us in the living room, Pooper started to howl. Dogs have sensitive hearing, and it was more than he could take.

I covered both of Pooper's ears. But I couldn't shut out the deafening snores.

"RRRRRHONNNNNK RRRRRRHHHHHHNNNNNNK!"
"RRRRRHONNNNNK RRRRRRHHHHHHNNNNNNK!"

The ceiling cracked some more.

"The noise—it's vibrating in my head! I . . . I feel sick!"

Luke Puke cried. He covered his mouth and went running to the bathroom.

"RRRRRHONNNNNK RRRRRRHHHHHHNNNNNNNK!"

Everyone came running out of their rooms.

"Earthquake!" Wacky Jackie yelled. "Everyone duck under a table!"

**"RRRRRHONNNNNK RRRRRRHHHHHHNNNNNNNK!
"RRRRRHONNNNNK RRRRRRHHHHHHNNNNNNNK!"**

"There's a *bear* in the house!" Babbling Brooke screamed. "Run for your lives!"

They couldn't escape from the hall—my stomach blocked their way. "There's no bear," I said. "It's Mama. She snores kind of loud."

"RRRRRHONNNNNK RRRRRRHHHHHHNNNNNNNK!"

The snores were so loud they even woke up Adam Bomb, who came staggering into the hall rubbing his head. "What's up? What's happening?" he asked.

It usually takes Adam a couple of days to recover after his head blows up. But even a headless kid couldn't stay asleep with those roaring snores shaking the house apart.

"Adam—it's Mama," I said. "She—"

CRRASSH!

We all jumped. Paintings were coming off the walls. I ducked as plaster fell from the ceiling and landed all around me.

"We've *got* to do something!" Nervous Rex cried, holding his ears.

"I have an idea," Handy Sandy said. "And I think it will work."

"What's your idea?" Brainy Janey asked.

"Close her door," Sandy said.

She and Janey crept up to Mama's bedroom. Silently and slowly, they pulled the door shut.

Would that make it quieter?

"RRRRRHONNNNNK RRRRRRHHHHHHNNNNNNK!"

No—Mama's bedroom door cracked off its hinges and fell to the floor.

"RRRRRHONNNNNK RRRRRRHHHHHHNNNNNNK!"

"My ears are *bleeding*!" Nervous Rex cried.

"What are we going to do?" Sandy asked.

Brainy Janey stepped up to the fallen bedroom door. "I have another idea," she said.

FORTY-TWO

Brainy Janey here, continuing the story . . .

We were all gathered in the dark hallway near Mama's bedroom. Each snore coming from her open mouth caused pain and destruction. We had to act fast.

"We have to let her know that she isn't wanted," I said. "Let's carry her bed out to the backyard as she sleeps. When she wakes up in the morning and sees she's outside, maybe she'll take the hint."

"Brilliant!" Brooke exclaimed. "Janey has done it again. Go, Janey! Go, Janey!"

Nervous Rex shook his head. "But if we take her outside, her snores will chase away all the birds and bunnies and squirrels. Besides, she'll wake up all the neighbors!"

"Worth it," I said. "She'll get the hint and realize she isn't wanted. And then she'll pack up and leave."

"RRRRRHONNNNNK RRRRRRHHHHHHHNNNNNNK!"

That blast from Mama sent Rex crashing into the wall. "Okay . . . let's try it," he said. So that's what we did.

First, we found earplugs in the bathroom. Then we crept into her room and surrounded her bed.

We were all working together. "Let's lift it now," I said. "Come on. On the count of three. One . . . two . . . three."

"Too heavy!" Cranky Frankie groaned.

"Too heavy. We can't lift it!" Adam Bomb cried.

"Way too heavy," Rob Slob agreed.

"RRRRRHONNNNNK RRRRRRHHHHHHHNNNNNNK!"

Mama stirred. Was she about to wake?

"We can't give up," I whispered.

"I have a plan!" Handy Sandy cried. "I know how we can do it." She disappeared. And a few seconds later she returned carrying four roller skates.

"Brilliant! We *skate* to the backyard!" Wacky Jackie declared.

Sandy frowned at her. "No. We don't wear the skates. The *bed* wears the skates. We put these under the bed legs and roll it outside."

"Brilliant!" Babbling Brooke cried. "Go, Sandy! Go, Sandy!"

It took a while to get the skates under the bed. Mama turned onto her side, but she didn't wake up.

Finally, we rolled the bed out into the hall. We made a sharp left turn and headed to the back.

"RRRRRHONNNNNK RRRRRRHHHHHHNNNNNNK!"

Snore after snore battered us. It was like we were being hit by ocean waves in a strong current.

"RRRRRHONNNNNK RRRRRRHHHHHHNNNNNNK!"

The sound made us weak. My head was ringing. Several times we almost slid the bed into the wall. But we made it outside and pushed the bed into the yard as Mama snored away.

"Okay, we're here!" I whispered. "We did it!"

We were so happy we made it outside without waking Mama up, we all wanted to celebrate. We cheered silently and pumped silent fists and did some crazy silent dancing. It was a great moment.

I turned and started to walk back to the house. But a shout made me stop and spin around.

"THE BED!" Adam Bomb cried. "IT'S ROLLING AWAY!"

I gasped as I saw the bed moving . . . and picking up speed as it bumped down our sloping yard.

"STOP IT!" Nervous Rex yelled. "SOMEBODY S-STOP IT!"

I clapped my hands over my cheeks. "Oh no!" I cried. "It's rolling into the STREET!"

FORTY-THREE

We all went chasing after the bed. But it didn't go very far—it crashed into a line of metal garbage cans at the curb.

The bed stopped.

We stopped.

"BRRRRRHHHHHHK."

And with a final snort, Mama sat up.

She blinked her eyes a few times, then stretched her arms above her head. Her face filled with surprise as she gazed around at the night sky, the streetlights, and the dark houses across the way.

We're in major trouble, I thought. *She's going to go berserk now. This isn't going to be pretty.*

We all gasped in surprise as a smile crossed her face. Then she turned and saw us for the first time.

"Fresh air!" she exclaimed. "I *love* fresh air."

None of us said a word. We didn't know what to say.

"Fresh air and peace and quiet," Mama said, still smiling. "My favorite things in the world."

Her smile grew even wider. "I love peace and quiet," she said. "You know, I once had a roommate who snored. Can you believe that? I had to kick her out of the house!"

I needed to think fast. "Yes, we thought you'd like it out here," I said.

Mama nodded. "Like it? I love it. And you dum-dum cluck-clucks will, too. Tomorrow, we're bringing *all* our beds outside. We're all going to sleep in the fresh air from now on!"

FORTY-FOUR

The next morning at breakfast, Mama kept talking about fresh air and peace and quiet and how much she loved it. "Peace and quiet," she said. "You can't have one without the other. Do you dum-dum drool-faces know what I mean?"

No one answered. We didn't know *what* she meant.

"Peace and quiet," Mama repeated. "That's the rule around here from now on."

Rob Slob said, "Please pass the salt." And she slapped him with her cane for making a racket.

Then Mama gobbled down all the pancakes. She ate with both hands, syrup dripping down her chin. And she didn't save any for us, either.

After breakfast, Handy Sandy pulled me aside. "I've invented the perfect thing to get rid of Mama," she said.

"You're the best inventor in the house," I said. "It's a shame your inventions never work."

"This one *will* work," Sandy said, and held up a towel.

"That's a bath towel," I said. "I know you didn't invent the bath towel, Sandy."

"Give me a chance to explain," Sandy said. "Yes, it's a bath towel. But I sewed a bear trap inside it."

"A bear trap? Like the one in the welcome mat?"

Sandy grinned. "Just like it. Only this time it will work. When Mama takes her shower, she'll grab the bath towel. And the trap will snap tight around her."

"Then what?" I said.

"Then she'll beg for help. And we say we'll only get her out of the trap if she agrees to leave."

I stared at the towel. "Hmmmm. Okay . . . I guess it's worth a try. I don't have any better ideas."

Sandy raised the towel. "I'll put it in Mama's shower. You'll see, Janey. This time I know it will—"

SSSNNNNAAAAAAAAAAAAP!

Sandy's eyes bulged, and her mouth flew open in a howl of pain. The towel clamped tightly around her body and she fell to the floor, kicking and screaming and gasping for breath.

"We need a new plan," I said. Later that day, I had a good one.

FORTY-FIVE

Welcome to our big Blast-Off Party.

We're going to send Mama off with a blast!

I invited everyone we know from Smellville Middle School. The idea is to come break the sound barrier with the loudest party in history. I'm hoping it will be so loud that moonlings can hear it on the moon!

I'm brainy, so I've done a lot of research on sound and sound waves.

I read that the human ear can only take about 220 decibobbles of sound before it explodes. I'm hoping that 500 decibobbles will be enough to make everyone's ears explode—and to chase Mama away from here forever!

Peace and quiet. That's all she talks about. She likes total silence, except when *she's* talking. She even tells us we *breathe* too loud.

So I got all our guests together and said, "It's party time. If we throw the loudest, rowdiest, most deafening, most ear-shattering party in history, Mama will go running."

Of course, everyone congratulated me on my brilliant plan.

And now here we were. Everyone came—and it was starting to get N-O-I-S-Y!

Some of the kids from school were doing their best Tarzan yells. And they got Pooper howling at the top of his lungs.

Another kid brought an old boom box—this gigantic music player. And he had it turned up to *infinity*. The music was making my heart leap into my mouth with each beat. It was so loud, we couldn't tell what kind of music was playing!

Babbling Brooke was leaping up and down shouting her cheers. Wacky Jackie was playing the bagpipes at full blast—they sounded like sour dog howls.

Luke Puke was off vomiting loudly in a corner. Nervous Rex's ears were bleeding!

Two kids I never saw before were playing tubas! They were so loud, I couldn't even hear Rob Slob and Junkfood John pounding their brains out on their drum sets!

BLAMAMABLAMMABLAMMMABLAMMMA!

Holding her ears, Handy Sandy came up to me and said something. Of course, I couldn't hear her.

She repeated herself, but I still couldn't hear. I took my earmuffs off. "WHAT IS IT?" I shouted.

BLAMAMABLAMMABLAMMMABLAMMMA!

"WHERE IS MAMA?" she shouted back.

I pointed to the back. "SHE'S IN HER ROOM."

"I HOPE SHE'S HATING ALL THE NOISE," Sandy screamed.

"I KNOW SHE IS," I said. "AFTER THIS PARTY, SHE'LL TAKE THE HINT AND SCRAM OUT OF HERE."

"YOU'RE SO BRAINY!" Sandy shouted.

"I KNOW," I said. Then an evil idea flashed into my overactive mind. "LET'S GO OPEN MAMA'S DOOR SO SHE CAN *REALLY* ENJOY THE PARTY!"

Sandy laughed and put her hand on my shoulder as we made our way down the hall to Mama's room.

BLAMAMABLAMMABLAMMMABLAMMMA!

The walls were shaking from the deafening racket, and the floor bounced under our feet.

"She's gonna be really *mad* !" Sandy said.

I grinned. "I sure hope so!"

Sandy and I stopped outside Mama's room and took a deep breath. Then we pushed open her door.

"Huh?" I gasped.

Sandy squeezed my arm. "Wha—?"

The room was empty. The bed was made. And there was no sign of Mama.

I gazed all around. "She isn't here?"

Then I spotted a white sheet of paper on the dresser. It was a note.

I picked it up and read it to Sandy:

> **So long, suckers.**
>
> **I'm outta here.**
>
> **I'm going to work for the Perfects.**
>
> **Penny and Parker Perfect hired me to be a perfectly bad example for their kids.**

The note trembled in my hand.

I turned to Sandy. "I—I—I"

We were speechless.

As we hurried back to the party, the powerful wave of sound crashed into us and we smashed against the wall.

BLAMAMABLAMMABLAMMMABLAMMMA!

I gritted my teeth, lowered my head, and staggered into the room.

"LISTEN UP!" I screamed. "LISTEN UP, EVERYONE! SHUT UP! EVERYONE, PLEASE SHUT UP!"

It took at least ten minutes to get everyone quiet.

Wacky Jackie refused to stop honking her bagpipes—Cranky Frankie finally had to wrestle the instrument away from her, then ripped it into pieces.

"The party is over!" I cried. "Mama is gone!"

A hush fell over the room.

"It worked," I told them. "She's gone. You can all go home now!"

More silence.

"Go home? Are you joking?" someone shouted. "We're *never* going home! *We're staying forever!*"

BLAMAMABLAMMABLAMMMABLAMMMA!

R.L. STINE has more than 400 million English-language books in print, plus international editions in thirty-two languages, making him one of the most popular children's authors of all time. Besides Goosebumps, he has written series including Fear Street, Rotten School, Mostly Ghostly, the Nightmare Room, Dangerous Girls, and Just Beyond. Stine lives in New York City with his wife, Jane, an editor and publisher.

JEFF ZAPATA has worked on comic books and trading cards for more than twenty-five years, including thirteen gross, memorable ones as an editor, art director, and artist on Garbage Pail Kids and other brands at the Topps Company.

JOE SIMKO is an artist known for his happy-horror style. He is one of the premiere Garbage Pail Kids illustrators for the Topps Company and lives in New York City with his wife, son, dog, and many, many boxes of cereal.

THE TOPPS COMPANY, INC., originator of Garbage Pail Kids, Mars Attacks, and Bazooka Joe brands, was founded in 1938 and is the preeminent creator and marketer of physical and digital trading cards, entertainment products, and distinctive confectionery.